THE ANTICIPATED SEQUEL TO *SCORPIO RISING*

THE STING OF THE SCORPIO

There Is a Fine Line Between Ambition and Greed

BY MASTER STORYTELLER
MONIQUE DOMOVITCH

If you purchased this book without a cover, you should be aware that this book is stolen property. It was reported as "unsold and destroyed" to the publisher, and neither the publisher not the author has received payment for this stripped book.

THE STING OF THE SCORPIO

Copyright © 2011 by Monique Domovitch.

This is a work of fiction. All of the characters, organizations, and events portrayed in this book are either a product of the author's imagination or are used fictitiously.

All rights reserved. No part of this book may be reproduced or transmitted in any form or by any means, electronic or mechanical, including photocopying, recording or by any information storage and retrieval system, without written permission from the author, except for the inclusion of brief quotations in a review.

Published by Lansen Paperback Publishing.

ISBN-13: 978-1466242340
ISBN-10: 1466242345

First Published October 2011

Dedication

*To my three girls,
Carol Ann, Rebecca and Alicia.
Thank you for encouraging and
believing in me when I needed it.*

Chapter 1

I am safe, thought Brigitte as the plane began its descent to New York.

It was only two weeks since she had married Alexander in the small ceremony at the Paris Hotel de Ville, and already her life had been turned completely upside down, some of it for the better, some of it...she wasn't sure.

She was surprised at the swirl of emotions she felt, staring at the immense city below. This was a move she would never have made alone, but luckily Alexander was with her—she glanced lovingly at him in the seat next to hers—as were her son, David and her friend and housekeeper, Réjeanne. So all was well, or so she wanted to believe.

She was landing in America, far from Paris and the threat of her stepfather. She still shuddered at the memory of Lucien standing in the doorway, his eyes wandering over her body as they had when she was just a child. She remembered the day he had reappeared as if it had been yesterday.

Réjeanne had taken one look at Brigitte's face and immediately known that something was terribly wrong. "Get out! Get out," she shouted at the old man as she tried to push him out the door.

He had shoved her aside easily and walked toward Brigitte "What's the matter Brigitte? Don't you recognize your own *papa*?" he asked.

Brigitte stood paralyzed with shock. "You're not my father. Get out of here," she said, her voice trembling with emotion.

The old man chuckled. "Aw, Brigitte, you're breaking my heart. Where's your gratitude for everything I did for you? It looks to me like you've done well for yourself. You're living in this fancy place, and with a maid. Seems to me you could show some gratitude to your father and help him out a bit in his old age."

From the back bedroom, Brigitte heard David laughing, and she prayed to God Lucien would leave before her son walked in. "How dare you come here?" Her voice was like ice. "You are nothing but a filthy bastard. Get out of here and don't ever come back."

Her words had seemed to delight Lucien. "You're calling me a bastard? Me? I think you've got that wrong *ma fille*. It's your son who is the bastard, not me. And I have a feeling I might have a pretty good claim to that little boy. As a matter of fact I have a feeling I might have as much right to him as you do."

That was when Brigitte had collapsed and Réjeanne screamed. From down the hall, Alex and David had come running.

Alex took one look at the scene before him and grabbed Lucien by the collar. "What the hell did you do to her?" he shouted.

"Hey! Take your hands off me. I didn't do a thing. I was just leaving." Lucien walked out, and from the doorway, called out menacingly, "You can tell her that I'll be back. That's my boy she's got there and unless she and I come to some agreement, she can expect to see me in court."

Brigitte shook her head, trying to rid herself of the memories. But she could not forget Réjeanne's and Alex's kindness when she confessed that Lucien was David's father.

Afterwards, Alex had taken her hand in his and said, "You have no reason to feel ashamed, Brigitte. The bastard raped you,." And rather than drive a wedge between them, her disclosure brought them closer.

The voice of the captain cut through her musings. "We hope you enjoyed your flight, and we thank you for using Pan Am."

The plane taxied down the runway, and a few minutes later Alexander held Brigitte's arm as they disembarked. She stepped down the portable stairs and turned to look at her husband, filled with an overwhelming rush of love for him. More than anything, she yearned to create the perfect family, the family she never had. *I will make him happy, she vowed. I will be the best wife I know how.*

But New York was alien. Everywhere she looked, she was surrounded by ugly grey buildings on city blocks the size of soccer fields. The streets were filthy. People looked angry, harassed, scared. They scowled at each other as they walked by. On the way from the airport, the cab stopped at a red light and a big black man with crazed eyes walked over to the car and stared openly at the occupants inside.

"Don't worry sweetheart, he's just another beggar." He rolled down the window and tossed a few coins to the man. A second later he had already moved on to the car behind. As Brigitte looked around at the unfamiliar city, she wondered if she could ever feel at home there.

Three weeks later, with Brigitte eager to move out of the rooming house where they had found temporary lodging, and into a place they could call home, Alex reluctantly signed a lease on an enormous loft in Greenwich Village. The building, an old warehouse, had been empty for over a year, and the owner was desperately trying to rent it.

"It isn't a residential building. I can't imagine how you can expect to live there," the agent told Brigitte when she expressed her interest in moving in. But he could not dissuade her. She loved the high ceilings, the large skylights, and the distinctly artistic community of the area, while the low rent agreed to Alexander's sense of economy.

"How are we going to turn this into a home?" Alex asked, slightly skeptical, as he walked around the vast expanse of dusty space.

"Leave that up to me, *mon chéri*," replied his new bride.

With her boundless energy and artist's flair,

Brigitte soon transformed it into a comfortable and functional home. The old hardwood floors were sanded and varnished. The brick walls were painted a flat white and the ceiling a starkly contrasting black. Stand-alone walls were built to provide privacy to the two bedrooms and the bathroom. The remaining space was left open, and once the industrial-size windows and the skylights were cleaned until they gleamed, the place was unrecognizable.

"*Et maintenant*, all we need is some color," declared Brigitte.

"It looks great already," agreed Alex, putting more conviction in his voice than he really felt. It still looked like an empty, albeit clean, warehouse to him. He wondered how his wife, who had left her luxurious apartment in Paris, could get excited over such a dump.

Brigitte was not finished. Over the next few weeks she found a variety of old, but solid second-hand furniture.

"You can't be serious," said Alex, getting close to the end of his confidence in the project. "I agreed to a loft because I know you need space and natural light for your studio. But I'll be damned if I agree to live like a pauper. This furniture is garbage. It's probably full of fleas."

"Don't be ridiculous. There is nothing wrong with this furniture. All it needs is new upholstery. You must trust me."

For days, samples of fabrics in dozens of colors hung from every available surface until Brigitte made the final selection. One morning a truck pulled up and all the old furnishings were carted away. Two weeks later they were brought back, looking like new.

The dusty old loft was unrecognizable. Huge screens in bright turquoise, sunny yellow, electric blue and bold pink, separated the living and the dining room from the kitchen area. One area was left totally bare, except for the professional size easel standing directly before the window. The space was to be Brigitte's studio.

From the ceiling hung long rows of black, funnel-shaped, light fixtures. Now recovered in shiny, white vinyl, looked new. Tropical plants filled every corner, and Brigitte's oils covered every spare inch of wallspace. The effect was electrifyingly modern.

Brigitte was triumphant. "*Voilà*," she said, jubilant. "Now what do you say?" she asked her husband.

"I say, you are a witch. A beautiful, talented, sexy witch." he took her in his arms.

From across the room, Réjeanne signaled to

David and led him away. "Let's go for a walk," she whispered to him. "I think your *Maman* and Alex want to be alone right now."

Brigitte was consumed with passion for her husband. He was her friend, her lover, her savior. Sometimes she wondered what might have happened if she had not phoned Alex and prevented him from flying away that day. She shuddered at the thought.

For weeks, she had avoided Alex's attentions. And then came the day she learned he was flying back to New York. If she hadn't picked up the phone and called him that day, God only knew what might have happened. One thing was sure. She would not be in New York any more than she would be his wife.

For the first time in a long time, she felt loved. Abandoning her career to follow Alex had been a small price to pay for what she now enjoyed, a loving marriage, and the reassuring knowledge that, at last, Lucien was out of her life forever. Since the wedding a few weeks ago, there had been no more nightmares.

Alex carried Brigitte to their room and threw her on the bed. "Alex, what are you doing?"

He unbuttoned her blouse and buried his face between her breasts. Brigitte laughed throatily. At the beginning, she had been terrified of sex. But slowly, gently, and ever so patiently, Alex had helped her overcome her fears. Not only had he not seemed to mind Brigitte's inexperience, but it appeared to excite him. Now, he found one of her nipples and sucked greedily. She moaned. "Oh God, Alex, I want you so much."

"I've created a monster," he said, chuckling. He pulled up her skirt and slipped his hand inside her panties. "I love you," he whispered in her ear.

Brigitte's knees went weak as a surge of desire filled her. She felt so much love she thought her heart might burst. "And you'll never love anybody else?"

"And I'll never love anybody else," he repeated dutifully as he climbed on top of her. A moment later he was inside her, moving at a deliciously slow pace, until Brigitte could no longer tell where her body ended and his began.

* * * * *

By day, while Brigitte struggled to adapt to life in New York, Alex fought his own battles. Since his carefree days in Paris had come to an end, reality had set in full force.

In Paris, falling in love with Brigitte and their quick decision to marry, had seemed like the best thing that had ever happened to him. Now, back in New York, it often felt more like insanity. *I'm only twenty-five years old. What am I doing with a wife and a son?* It wasn't that he didn't love his wife. He was still completely captivated by her. And although he couldn't think of a single woman he would rather make love to, he missed the feeling of being free. Occasionally, he remembered the vows he had spoken on their wedding day, 'forsaking all others,' and he felt…trapped!

Also weighing heavily on his mind, were his new financial responsibilities. It had been months since his last pay check, and he now had an extended family to support. Although Brigitte had insisted on helping financially, he had been adamant about being the sole provider.

"Don't you understand?" he argued with her. "I don't want your money. I am your husband. What kind of a husband would I be if I allowed my wife to pay the bills?"

"But Alex, I really don't mind. We're married now. The least I can do is help until you find a job."

"Absolutely not. I won't have it."

Brigitte had grudgingly conceded. Over the next few months, Alex watched helplessly as his bank account, which he had so painstakingly grown to a sizable sum, dwindled steadily. His sense of urgency rose.

Every day, rain or shine, while Brigitte busied herself with her new home, Alex continued his search for work. He studied the classifieds daily, applied at every employment agency and mailed countless resumes. He even swallowed his pride and went back to see William Brandon, his old boss.

To his immense relief, he did not run into Anne Turner. At her desk was an efficient looking middle-aged secretary, who gazed at him with professional disinterest and ordered him to sit and wait.

"Mr. Brandon is busy. I'll see if he has a minute for you," she told him and left him stewing in the reception area while she hurried down the hall to Brandon's office. Alex looked around. Nothing in the reception area had changed. The same expensive paintings hung on the walls, the same classical music played softly from the hi-fi. It was almost as though he had never left.

A voice suddenly broke through his thoughts. "Alex, what the hell are you doing here, you old son of a gun?" It was Ben, one of the guys from the bull pen they had nicknamed, 'purgatory'. "I thought you had decided to stay in Europe indefinitely."

Alex chuckled. "Naw, life was too hard there. Who can take all that fine wine and *French food*? Give me a good old hamburger anytime. Is Andrew around?"

"Didn't you hear? Andrew left months ago."

Before Ben could say anymore, the secretary reappeared. "Mr. Brandon will see you now." Alex hurried down the hall to the executive office.

William Brandon sat back in his chair, puffing away at his eternal cigar. He looked at Alex with distaste. "Well, if it isn't the wonder boy. You didn't do too well in Paris, did you? What makes you think you can just waltz back into your old job?"

Alex struggled with his ego for a few seconds. He needed this job. And then he saw the amusement in Brandon's eyes. The fucking bastard was enjoying his discomfort.

He turned and walked out.

• • • • •

Chapter 2

In the end, it was Brigitte who came up with the idea.

"Did you know that this building is for sale?" she asked over dinner one night.

They were alone in the dining area. Réjeanne had pleaded fatigue, put David to bed and retired. Now, Alex stared glumly at the *boeuf bourgignon* growing cold on his plate.

"Is it?" asked Alex, with disinterest. He picked up his fork and speared at his food. "What good does that do me? I don't have a job. And according to my last interview, I'm overqualified.

It seems nobody will pay me the kind of salary a person of my experience should get."

Brigitte ignored his comment and said, "How much would this apartment normally be worth?"

He put down his fork and looked at her blankly. "What are you talking about?"

She gestured to the room around them, and said, "Supposing we rented a place like this, one where we hadn't done all the renovations ourselves; how much could we expect to pay?"

"A hell of a lot more than we're paying now, that's for sure."

"How much more?"

He groaned with impatience. "How would I know? Double. Maybe triple. Why?"

"And how much did the renovations cost?"

"Very little actually," he answered. "I got all of the materials wholesale and I did most of the work myself."

Brigitte smiled victoriously. "I have an idea," she said and launched eagerly into her proposal.

Alex stayed up long into the night, going over the figures. He couldn't quite admit that Brigitte's idea was brilliant, but he just might be able to pull it off. The down payment alone would take up nearly all of his savings. And every last dime that remained would go toward the renovations. He would be left with no income and no savings. Without a job, how the hell would he get a bank to grant him a mortgage? By the time he climbed into bed, exhausted, the sun was already rising.

Brigitte stirred and opened one eye. "So, do you think we can do it?" she asked sleepily.

"I don't know. I'll have to think about it some more," he answered. He gave her a quick kiss, rolled over and fell asleep.

The next day he got on the telephone. After half a dozen calls, he finally located his friend Andrew McGregor.

"Why the hell didn't you call me sooner?" asked Andrew when he heard Alex's voice. "How long have you been back in town?"

"Not long, and I've been pretty busy. I have a wife and a son," he told him. "And now I'm looking for work." Alex could imagine his friend's freckled face grinning happily.

"What! You have a wife? Well for Chrissake! When am I going to meet the lady?" then he realized what else his friend had said. "Wait a minute. How could you have a son? Last time I saw you was only about six or seven months ago."

Alex made up a story about David being Brigitte's son from a previous marriage. "Why don't you come over for dinner Friday night?" Alex asked afterwards. "I'd like you to meet Brigitte. I know you'll love her."

The following Friday, Andrew arrived punctually at seven, with a bottle of Dom Perignon.

"This certainly deserves a celebration."

He kissed Brigitte on the cheek and gave David a playful slap on the back. "I never saw anyone with hair redder than mine." He turned back to Alex. "I must admit that the color looks better on your wife than on me." He leaned forward, whispering, "She's gorgeous. No wonder you kept her all to yourself."

They sat and enjoyed a dinner of *coq au vin*— Réjeanne's specialty. They popped open the bottle of champagne, and during the meal Alex brought Andrew up to date with his situation.

"You should have called me as soon as you came back," said Andrew. "You don't have to look any further. I have a job for you. You can start tomorrow if you like."

""What do you mean?" Alex didn't dare hope.

"I started my own company after leaving

Brandon & Associates." At the baffled look on Alex's face, Andrew explained. "My father agreed to back me financially." He chuckled. "Don't get the wrong idea. I'm not rolling in dough. The old man lent me the absolute minimum I needed to buy a tiny parcel of land at the outskirts of the city. That's where I plan to build a small residential project. And you, my friend, are exactly the person I need. Keep in mind I can't afford to pay much, but if you want it, the job is yours."

"Do I want it?" exclaimed Alex eagerly. "When do I start?"

* * * * *

A few days later it was official. With the confirmation of employment in his pocket, Alex put in an offer to purchase the building.

Brigitte was putting the final touches to a new painting when Alex burst in. He ran to her, picked her up in his arms, and twirled her around the room, almost knocking down her easel in the process. "Alex, *pour l'amour de Dieu*, put me down. What is going on?"

He pulled away from her. "You are looking at your new landlord," he said, beaming.

"Wh-what? Why didn't you tell me? When did this happen?"

"I signed the papers this morning. I wanted to surprise you."

"Well you did. You certainly did," said Brigitte. But she was not at all surprised. She knew that Alex had a brilliant mind and that someday her husband would be successful. This was only his first small step.

* * * * *

Alex settled back into working his twelve hour days with enthusiasm. This was the lifestyle he knew best and enjoyed most. He rose early in the morning and worked all day by Andrew's side, drawing plans for inexpensive but well constructed houses. This was a far cry from his old dream of developing luxury buildings, but at least he was earning a living, and the job gave him some measure of financial safety.

Evenings he came home to a quick dinner, and then spent the rest of the evening renovating his building. Worried that her husband was working too hard, Brigitte tried to ease his load by helping as much as she could. During the day she ran his errands, ordered the long lists of building materials needed for the renovations. She supervised the electricians and plumbers, quickly learning the difference between good and shoddy work. Often, she surprised the workers by pulling on overalls and joining them in plastering and sanding. Being an artist, she enjoyed painting along with her husband, sometimes until she thought her arms would fall off. Even with their combined efforts, it often seemed the renovations would never end. Most nights they crawled into bed so exhausted they had no energy left for talking, let alone lovemaking.

"Why don't we take the weekend off?" asked Brigitte one morning over breakfast. "We could relax for a change; maybe go out to dinner and a movie."

Alex was gulping down his coffee in his usual rush. "Sorry sweetheart. I wish I could, but I just don't have the time. I have some plans to finish for Andrew, and there's still too much work to do on the downstairs apartment."

Brigitte hesitated. "Alex, I hardly see you anymore, unless it's when we're working. I miss you. David misses you. Couldn't you find some time, maybe just one evening a week, for us?"

Alex looked up at her, scowling. "Really Brigitte, don't you think you're exaggerating. I come home every single night. When I'm not home, I'm working. I have to finish that apartment and rent it fast. Do you think I'm made of money or something? I can't afford to keep paying the mortgage on this building without getting rent from at least one apartment soon. I would like your support, instead of this constant nagging."

Brigitte swallowed her disappointment and saw him off with her usual warm kiss. After Alex left, Brigitte sat and thought for a long time. Whatever she had expected of married life, this was not it. Sometimes she almost regretted having told him her idea of buying this building. She knew that Alex was serious about creating a successful career for himself, and she appreciated his efforts, but she missed the quiet times they used to spend together, talking and cuddling. *I hardly see my husband anymore.*

• • • • •

During those first months in the unfamiliar city, David became Brigitte's only solace. *I don't know what I would do without him.* Every morning, after Alex left for work, Brigitte prepared breakfast for her son and played with him until it was time to leave for school, and then they would walk together the few blocks to Saint Martin's Academy, where David was registered in first grade. Luckily, David had adapted to his new country more easily than his mother. From the first day, Brigitte had employed a tutor to help him with his English and within a short time, he was fluent.

"I can hardly believe it," had exclaimed the teacher after the first week. "That child has an incredible memory. Once he's heard a word, he never forgets it. And his accent is almost perfect."

That's my bright boy, thought Brigitte proudly. "I wish I could get rid of my accent as easily."

"Oh, no! On you it's very attractive," replied the tutor. "Don't even try to lose it."

Brigitte smiled gratefully at the elderly man. It was the first compliment she had received in a long time. *Alex hardly seems to notice me anymore.*

Brigitte enjoyed every moment she spent with her son. Even after the endless hours of work she did on the suites downstairs, sanding and painting, varnishing and polishing day after day, she still had more freedom than she ever enjoyed in her life. After so many years of having precious little time to devote to David, she delighted in the luxury of spending long, delicious hours with her son.

Most of all, Brigitte was thrilled to discover in David a gift for art. At the end of his school day, David would rush back home, eager to pick up his mother's paints and brushes.

"He spends hours at my easel," said Brigitte to Alex one night, freeing her hair from the hair band and brushing out a few pieces of plaster.

Alex had come home earlier than usual that evening and Brigitte quickly changed out of her paint splattered overalls before showing him her son's latest effort.

"He has a good eye and he's good with a brush. Look at this. The composition is wonderful. The colors are good. Even his use of shadows is amazing."

Alex glanced at the painting and then turned back to Brigitte, shaking his head. "You coddle him. The boy should be outside getting some fresh air, playing with kids his own age. You shouldn't keep him cooped up all the time."

Brigitte was hurt at her husband's lack of enthusiasm. "Alex, for goodness sake. David can't play sports. He has a heart condition." She had repeated this so many times, she couldn't bring herself to tell him about David's epilepsy.

"I don't want to argue with you," answered Alex irritably. "But you know as well as I do that he needs to be active. Running around in the sunshine would do him a hell of a lot more good than keeping him cooped up inside, playing with paint. He needs to get stronger. Don't get me wrong, David is a great kid, but he's much too dependent on you."

He's jealous, realized Brigitte, shocked. The thought had flashed through her mind so quickly that she wondered if she had said it out loud.

"Alex," she said gently. "I'm still adapting to living in New York and so is David. It's normal that we spend a lot of our time together. Of course I love him, he's my son, but that doesn't take away from my feelings for you. I wish you and I could spend more time together too. But you are always so busy we never seem to be together anymore."

Alex was silent for a moment. "Sometimes, I just don't understand you Brigitte. I married you, and I come home every night? Isn't that enough? Here I am, working myself to the bone, trying to earn a good living for you and your son, and rather than appreciate me, you make me feel guilty."

The words cut through Brigitte like knife, making her feel like an ungrateful child. *How can he say that when I try so hard to be understanding and supportive.*

* * * * *

One month later, the last coat of varnish on the wood floors had dried, and the first apartment was ready to rent. Determined to reduce Alex's load in any way she could, Brigitte placed the ads in the neighborhood paper herself, and over the next few days, she showed the apartment to dozens of prospective tenants. By the end of the week, it was rented.

That evening Brigitte put on a clingy black dress, piled her hair high on top of her head and sprayed herself with perfume. When Alex walked in later that night, she greeted him at the door with glass of wine in one hand and a check from the new tenants in the other.

In bed later, sated from the first lovemaking they'd had in a long while, Alex leaned over his wife, brushing a wisp of her red hair off her face, and said, "I'd almost forgotten what a beautiful wife I have."

Brigitte knew that his amorous mood had been greatly inspired by his relief that the downstairs apartment was bringing in money, at last.

She smiled and said, "The rental income will more than cover the mortgage payments. What should we to do with the rest of the money?" She was dreaming of a short holiday just for the two of them. This was the perfect opportunity to get away and fall in love all over again. Besides, they hadn't been on a real honeymoon yet.

"We'll pay the mortgage with part of it," answered Alex. He was staring at an invisible spot on the ceiling, his eyes shining with excitement. "And the rest, we'll bank. Someday, I want to own a hundred buildings like this one."

"My husband—a regular King Midas," she said with a sigh.

"What are you talking about?" asked Alex sleepily.

"Haven't you heard of the story of the King who turned everything he touched to gold?" she asked.

"Sounds great."

"Oh yes," she continued. "Until one day, he touched his daughter by mistake and she turned into a golden statue and... Alex, are you sleeping?"

Alex's deep, regular breathing was her answer.

For a long time Brigitte lay in the dark, thinking. The last thing she wanted was to prevent Alex from achieving his dreams. But lately she had come to feel totally unimportant to him. Her husband seemed to have time for everything but for her. She immediately felt guilty. *I refuse to become a whiny, nagging wife. I will just have to keep myself busy. Maybe I should resume my own career.* She turned to her side and looked at her sleeping husband. "I do love you," she whispered softly. "Very, very much."

• • • • •

Anne Turner turned the key and walked into her apartment. As soon as she stepped in, she was assailed by the piercing cries of the infant. "Shut up!" she snapped. "I was only gone a couple of hours." *Damn! I can't even take a break without that kid waking up the whole neighborhood.* She went to the kitchen and pulled a baby bottle out of the refrigerator. Without bothering to heat it, she hurried to the bedroom and shoved the nipple into her son's mouth. "There, that'll shut you up for awhile."

She tucked a pillow under the bottle so it would stay up by itself. She watched the baby as he fed. Lately her luck had taken a turn for the worse. She had given up on trying to locate Alex Ivanov. As far as she knew he was still in Paris working on some project. *He was never a good prospect anyhow. I want a man with money and lots of it.* But since her pregnancy, she had been unable to find a single decent prospect. *Rich men don't want mistresses with kids of their own. They want fresh young things with small waists and perfect breasts.* She looked down at the sucking baby. "Damn that Alex Ivanov for knocking me up and then dumping me," she said, conveniently forgetting that it was she who had seduced and then discarded him as an unworthy suitor.

* * * * *

CHAPTER 3

In Greenwich, the Black Cat Café was a Mecca of sorts to artists, flower children, hippies, hip singers, actors, and socialites alike. Although the small restaurant was tucked away in the back of an alley, it was always crowded.

Natalia Berenson sat at her usual window seat, savoring the last spoonful of her *soupe du jour*. Then she carefully wiped the bowl with a piece of bread which she ate with relish. Natalia was a bright and bubbly middle-aged woman, with a body somewhat reminiscent of Disney's Hippo in a Tutu. Her hair was platinum blonde and her voice sounded like a cross between James Cagney's and Mae West's—low, husky and gravelly all at once. She wore more makeup than a Las Vegas showgirl and enough diamonds to compete with DeBeers.

There had been a time, some years ago—before she gained all the weight and before cigarettes disguised her voice—when Natalia Berenson had been a glamorous movie star. During her short but illustrious career, she had married seven times, six of which were to very wealthy men, and had once been quoted as saying that unfortunately, her marriages were mistakes, but her divorces had more than made up for them. This comment was made shortly after her most successful divorce, which left her, as she put it to a journalist, 'disgustingly rich, dahhhrling'.

But unfortunately for Natalia, she had soon after, married and divorced number seven, who as it turned out, was even worse in divorce than he had been in marriage. After one short and tumultuous year of marriage, during which number seven had swindled her out of her fortune and run off with a girl half her age and one quarter of her size, Natalia had remained devotedly single. Now, ten years later, she pursued friendships with the same passion she used to display for finding husbands. She surrounded herself with friends running the gamut from interesting but impoverished, to the very rich and very famous.

Natalia sighed with satisfaction and pushed away her bowl. Now that her appetite was satisfied, she was free to pursue her other favorite activity, people watching. Her attention focused on the beautiful redhead sitting a few tables away. *Ah, there she is—the artist.* She had first noticed her a few days earlier. Although the girl's mass of red hair was splattered with speckles of paint and seemed in dire need of a good trim, Natalia had detected the girl's proud bearing and intelligent eyes. There was something special about her, she had decided. Over the next few days, Natalia had entertained herself by guessing the girl's background. She was an Irish lassie, come to New York to find her one true love. She was a German princess in hiding from her royal duties. *Ah, Natalia*, the woman told herself, *you truly are an incurable romantic.* But, as she well knew, other people's romances were the only ones she was likely to have, so she indulged in these fantasies as much as she wanted.

Natalia watched now, as the girl pulled open a sketch pad and began to draw. There was a concentration about her, the kind of focus one usually found in passionate and talented artists. *When she works, nothing else exists. She doesn't even hear the people around her.* Oddly, the same comment could have been made about Natalia when she people watched. Natalia signaled for the waiter. He came running over. "Yes, Miss Berenson?"

"You see that girl over there?" she said, pointing to the redhead.

"Yes," he answered hesitantly.

"Would you be so kind as to ask her to come over?" It wasn't a request. It was a royal command from one of Hollywood's greatest legends. The boy hurried over to Brigitte, who was drawing in a large sketchbook.

Since David had started school a few months earlier, Brigitte had fallen into the habit of stopping by the Black Cat Café every morning for a coffee. Here the *croissants* were light and flaky, the *café au lait* rich and creamy, and unlike most other restaurants where only salted butter was served, at The Black Cat, the butter was sweet, just as it was in Europe. Those were only a few of the small things that Brigitte missed about Paris, but here, when she closed her eyes, she could almost believe herself back in France.

The waiter hurried over and whispered a few words in her ear. Brigitte looked across the room at Natalia Berenson. For some reason, the overly made-up woman with the painted eyebrows and thethick false eyelashes seemed hauntingly familiar. Her curiosity piqued, she picked up her cup of coffee, her sketch pad and pencils, and walked over. "You wanted to speak to me?"

"Yes, would you care to join me?" asked Natalia, nodding to the waiter to pull a chair.

She waited for Brigitte to sit before continuing. "I hope you'll forgive my rudeness. My legs are not as strong as they used to be. It is much easier to ask others to join me than for me to join them." She laughed and her massive body quivered like jelly. "Don't tell me... you're an artist," she continued, falling into one of her favorite roles, a fortuneteller she had played in a movie years ago. She closed her eyes and continued. "And you're not American. You're definitely European." Natalia's eyes popped open and swept over Brigitte, noting every detail of her makeup, of her dress. "You can only be from Paris. Am I right?"

"How did you know?"

She shrugged, delighted. "It's a game I play with myself. Whenever I see someone interesting, I try to guess everything about that person." She chuckled. "Besides, your accent gave you away. Just as you are a very good artist, I am very good at guessing people." Her eyes sharpened as she studied Brigitte. "Am I right? Are you very good?"

Brigitte hesitated for a second, and then nodded. "Yes. I am."

Natalia smiled and leaned back in her chair. It creaked dangerously. "I like that. You have no false humility. Let me see. You are a Virgo and you came to New York for love."

Brigitte laughed. "You are right."

"What sign is your lover?"

"My lover? Oh, you mean my husband. He is Scorpio."

"Hmm. Scorpio man and Virgo woman are a good match. They complement each other. But you must never give up your own power. Scorpios lust for power and will devour those who are weaker than them." Abruptly, she changed the subject. "Show me what you have." She gestured toward the sketchpad.

Normally, Brigitte would never have agreed to show her sketches. They were no more than scribbles, works in progress, but something about Natalia's bearing inspired confidence and respect. Brigitte liked her. She picked up her sketch book and handed it over.

Natalia flipped quickly through the pages, pausing for a second here and there. She closed the book and handed it back to Brigitte. "Very impressive," she said. "I expected as much. Who is your agent?"

"I don't have one yet." And seeing the woman's eyebrows shoot up, she felt compelled to explain.

"In Paris I was with Le Gallet. I've only arrived in New York a few months ago. I didn't want to approach anyone until I have enough paintings for an exhibition."

"I want to see everything you have, and I want to see it right now," said Natalia.

"Right now? But, I…my husband…" Without thinking, Brigitte heard herself say, "Could you come tomorrow morning?" And before she knew it, she and Natalia had a firm appointment for the next day.

The next morning, after spending half the night cleaning and rearranging furniture, Brigitte guided Natalia throughout the apartment. She showed the actress a picture of David, and introduced her to Réjeanne. Both women were in their early fifties, but there was a world of difference between them. Although Natalia was obese, she oozed glamour and looked years younger than her age. Réjeanne, on the other hand, was round and prematurely grey, and looked like a cuddly grandmother.

As soon as Réjeanne heard Natalia's name, she went into near hysterics. "*Oh mon Dieu, mais c'est* Natalia Berenson, the movie star. I have seen every one of your movies. Please, may I have your autograph?" She ran for a pen and a piece of paper and handed them over for the movie star's signature with trembling hands.

"I'm sorry. I had no idea you were somebody famous," said Brigitte after Réjeanne backed out of the room, nearly bowing in adoration of her favorite American actress. "I didn't recognize you."

Natalia shrugged. "You were just a child at the time. Besides, I've changed a lot since my movie days," she said. "Now show me your paintings."

The film star examined each painting carefully, peering at them from up close, and then backing up a few steps to study them from a distance. Afterward she nodded and said, "I'd like somebody else to take a look at them. Would you mind?"

"Not at all," replied Brigitte, slightly in awe of her famous guest. "It will be my pleasure."

* * * * *

A few days later, Daniel Drucker called for an appointment. "Natalia Berenson asked me to call," he said, sounding slightly irritated. "I don't have much time, but I just got a cancellation. I have some time afternoon." A few hours later he stopped by, looking sullen and preoccupied.

DD, as he asked to be called, was a tall, effeminate man with a mane of curly blond hair and an aristocratic bearing. He raced through the apartment as though he couldn't get out of there fast enough.

"Here are my paintings," said Brigitte, guiding him to the area she called the dining room. "I like that one," he said, pointing to the oil on the furthest wall and sounding bored.

"Thank you. I like it too," said Brigitte, wondering what exactly Natalia had in mind when she put DD in touch with her.

DD studied each painting, and then walked over to the dining room again, this time carefully examining every piece of artwork on the surrounding walls. "They're not bad. Not bad at all." He continued throughout the apartment, stopping here, pausing there, but never for more than a few seconds. "So that's all you have to show? Half a dozen oils?"

Brigitte shook her head. "Most of my work is over here." She guided him to the studio area. Behind her, DD gasped in surprise. He took his glasses off his nose, polished them with a silk handkerchief, put them back on and stared reverently at a large rendering of a flea-market scene. "This is absolutely divine," he said. He moved on to a colorful still life and gazed at it in wonder. Brigitte could sense his excitement. She held her breath. At last he turned back to her and said, "Miss Dartois, please forgive me for doubting your talent. I should have known that Natalia would never have recommended you unless you were truly gifted." He pulled out a card from the breast pocket of his jacket and handed it to Brigitte with a flourish. "I would be honored if you allowed me to do a showing of your work."

Brigitte could barely hold back her enthusiasm. "Yes, yes, of course."

The moment Alex arrived that night, she told him about the meeting. "And he wants to represent me," she added.

Alex listened, quietly, as he sipped his glass of wine. "I hope you don't jump into this without giving it some thought. Singing up with an agent, preparing for an exhibition, those are things that will affect our lives."

"But, I was already an artist when we met. And of course I want to paint again. I said yes, Alex."

This was not what he wanted to hear, but all he said was, "As long as you're happy, sweetheart, that's all that counts." And then he contradicted himself by adding, "I wish you had consulted me before agreeing. Are you sure you want to deal with this man? You have no idea who he is. He could be a fake for all you know."

Brigitte smiled and refilled his glass. "Alex, I'm a nobody in New York. I'm lucky he agreed to represent me," she said. "Natalia Berenson recommended him. Why would she recommend him unless he was excellent in his field?"

"I suppose," he said, not sounding convinced.

"By the way, Natalia has invited us to a cocktail party on Friday night."

Alex grumbled and set down his glass on the coffee table. "I have a lot of work to do. I can't just drop everything to go to some stupid party."

"Please Alex." She looked at him pleadingly. Although he had not said as much, his body language made it clear he was unhappy with her news, but for the life of her, she couldn't understand why. "We hardly ever go anywhere. A party would be fun."

He shrugged, scowling. "Tell you what, you go on ahead and I'll join you later."

Brigitte knew that small compromise was the most she would get. She threw her arms around him. "Thank you *mon chéri*. I promise you, we'll have a great time."

⁎ ⁎ ⁎ ⁎ ⁎

On the night of the party, Brigitte slipped into a sleek, black cocktail dress and put her hair up in a smooth chignon. She applied her makeup carefully, painting on eyeliner with practiced strokes and brushing her lips with her favorite red. It would be the first time she and Alex went out since their arrival in New York and she wanted her husband to be proud of her.

At the appointed time, Brigitte took a cab over to the lower east side where the party was being held in a dark and cavernous warehouse. She walked into the decrepit building, her eyes noticing the cigarette butts strewn all over the floor. Her ears slowly adjusted to the deafening music blasting from the large speakers. The rhythm reverberated through her body until her insides vibrated. Natalia held court at the entrance. She was decorated in all her finery and dripping in diamonds. She greeted each guest effusively, handing them a glass of champagne and then sending them merrily into the crowded darkness beyond.

From the doorway, Brigitte squinted into the madness inside. There were men in formal attire, others in jeans. Women wore anything from elaborate evening gowns to tight jeans and completely see-through blouses. Her brows jumped up at the sight of one girl wearing nothing but a minuscule pair of gold *lamé* panties and gold body-spray. Never in her life had Brigitte ever witnessed such a scene.

"Brigitte," Natalia exclaimed when she noticed her. "I'm so glad you could come. Where's Alex?"

"He had some work to finish. He'll be here later," Brigitte shouted over the blasting music.

Natalia rolled her eyes. "It's too bad he's not here. I could introduce him to a dozen people who could be of great help to him. You tell him that when you go home."

"You can tell him yourself. He promised he'd be here later."

An attractive man with salt and pepper hair and blue eyes, stood next to Natalia. Brigitte could feel his eyes on her. "Hi, I'm Gerald Masson," he introduced himself. "You must be the artist Natalia has told me so much about. What she forgot to mention was how beautiful you are."

Natalia laughed sending her entire body quivering and her diamonds dancing. "Please excuse my manners. Gerald is a very dear friend of mine. He doesn't usually like parties. I had to twist his arm." Before Brigitte could say anything, Natalia waved her on ahead. "Have fun, darling." As soon as she was out of ear shot, Natalia turned back to Gerald Masson, watching him intently. "Let me warn you, my darling. Brigitte is married and very much in love with her husband."

"Don't worry, Natalia," replied Gerald Masson, with no hesitation. "Since Kate passed away, I have not had the slightest inclination to get involved again."

Natalia patted his arm sympathetically. "You still miss her, don't you?" she asked.

Gerald Masson did not hesitate. "Every moment of every day," he admitted.

Brigitte looked around the packed room. In the middle was a small stage on which people danced with abandon. The atmosphere was one of merry madness, but she felt unable to join in the fun. She circled the room, pausing here and there to accept a hors d'oeuvre or a glass of wine. She felt lonelier in the joyful crowd than she did by herself at home. *I wish Alex would get here*, she thought. Suddenly, she felt a hand on her arm, and she turned around happily. "Alex—" she began and stopped. Gerald Masson was smiling down at her. "Oh, it's you," she said breathlessly.

"Sorry to disappoint you. You were expecting someone else?"

Brigitte quickly regained her composure. "I'm sorry. For a moment I thought you were my husband."

"I saw you looking bored," said Gerald. "And I thought you might like some company."

"I-I don't know anyone here, except for Natalia, and she's busy being the hostess," explained Brigitte, feeling embarrassed. "But I'd like to dance if you don't mind," she added, peeking up to meet his eyes, and then dropping her gaze to his shoes, suddenly embarrassed at her forwardness.

"It will be my pleasure," replied Gerald Masson as he escorted her to the center of the floor.

For the rest of the evening, Gerald Masson gently but efficiently took command. When the music changed from rock to a slow number, he gallantly guided her off the floor and introduced her to a few people. Whenever her glass needed refilling, Gerald immediately saw to it, and Brigitte did not have a dull moment.

From a distance, one of the fashionably gaunt guests approached Natalia. "Who is that red head in the black dress with Gerald Masson?" she asked, breathless with curiosity.

Natalia, instantly on guard, smiled benignly. "Lovely isn't she?" she answered easily. "Unfortunately my dear, there's no gossip there. She's Brigitte Dartois, a very talented artist I've recently discovered. She's also very married. Her husband couldn't come until later. Gerald is simply being courteous until he arrives."

The woman continued eagerly. "My goodness, what a shock I had when I first saw her. She looks just like Kate. For a moment, I almost thought she was Kate. I can't imagine what Gerald is doing with her. Of all people, he must be aware of the uncanny resemblance."

"Really Daphne, you are exaggerating. The only similarity between Brigitte and his wife is their hair color. Now if you'll excuse me, I must speak to Arnold," she said, hurrying away. *I refuse to play along with that woman's quest for gossip. Gerald Masson has suffered enough*, she thought, crossing the room in search of the nonexistent Arnold. *The last thing Gerald needs is Daphne Morris to make up some ridiculous story about him.*

The party was ending. Guests were leaving, and Alex had never arrived. Although Brigitte tried valiantly to cover her disappointment, Gerald Masson had been aware of her growing frustration. He turned to Brigitte. "Would you like me to drive you home?" he asked. "My car is right outside."

"Are you sure...if it's not out of your way."

"I'm absolutely sure. And I insist," he said, directing her toward the exit.

Gerald helped her into the passenger seat of an impeccably-kept, late model Jaguar, and then crossed over to the driver's side. "You'll have to direct me," he said, turning the key in the ignition.

The drive was short but pleasant, and Brigitte found herself relaxing in the company of this quiet man. Once in a while, she could feel his eyes on her in the dark and had the strange impression that he was on the verge of saying something. But whatever it was, he kept to himself. When the car pulled up in front of her building, he hopped out of the car and helped her out.

Brigitte turned to face him. "Thank you. If I had a good time tonight, it was entirely because of you."

"That's kind of you to say," he answered, and

hesitated for a moment. "You are a very lovely lady. Your husband is a lucky man," he said and returned to his car.

Just before he left, Brigitte had a disconcerting thought. *I wonder how his lips would feel*, she wondered, and then she hurried inside, feeling guilty. *What is the matter with me? A man pays me a small compliment, and I get all silly. I am a married woman with a wonderful husband.*

A few minutes later when Brigitte walked into her bedroom, she was astounded to find Alex fast asleep under the covers. *He didn't even try. He let me wait for him all evening and he didn't even try to come.*

She tiptoed out of the bedroom and changed quietly in the bathroom.

* * * * *

CHAPTER 4

In his penthouse, high above the city, Gerald Masson stared out below at the view of Central Park. It seemed like only yesterday that he and Kate had strolled together along Central Park. *Could it be that ten years have gone by since I asked her to marry me?* He closed his eyes to better remember that day.

They had spent the Sunday in the park, stopping at the fountain at the top of the hill. Kate was talking about a documentary she had seen, too excited to notice him retrieve the ring from his pocket until he held it out in front of her.

"Will you make me the happiest man in the world and marry me, Kate?"

The Sting of the Scorpio

She had thrown her arms around him and shouted, "Yes, yes, yes," all the while tears were running down her face. It was only after they had resumed their walk that Gerald had realized that some of the moisture on his face was from tears of his own. Next to their wedding day, it had been the happiest of his life; and for nine short years he'd had the privilege of loving the most wonderful woman in the world—until the cancer took her away. He swallowed hard, remembering her last few months. Since her death one year ago, he had been convinced that he could never love again. Until tonight. Until Brigitte Ivanov.

"I'm sorry Kate," he whispered in the darkness. But somehow, he felt peaceful. *I know you understand*. The last thing she had said to him before closing her eyes that last time was that she wanted him to love again.

"She's so much like you, my darling," he whispered to the silence in the room. *I just wish she wasn't attached*.

* * * * *

Over the last few months, Alex's discomfort with being married continued to grow. Although he had a wife he loved, he had no idea how to be a husband. He would have liked to be a happily married man and rush home to his loving wife at the end of every day, but he felt resentful and trapped. *I love my wife*, he told himself daily, almost like a mantra. *But I'm not the domestic type. She has to understand that I need to make something of myself.* To compound his confusion, Alex also realized that as much as he was uncomfortable with Brigitte's efforts to help him with his project, he resented even more her decision to pursue her own career. *Why is it that caring for David and me isn't enough for her?* He swallowed his displeasure and said nothing. Bitterly, he watched Brigitte become busier. Every time he turned around, Natalia Berenson was throwing another cocktail party, inviting Brigitte to yet another social occasion.

"Socializing is an important part of building my career," explained Brigitte. Alex never prevented her from going, but he also never joined her. And to Alex's mounting resentment, Brigitte's career began to take off.

It was after midnight, Brigitte was reading in bed when Alex stumbled in. "DD sold my first painting today. Isn't it wonderful?"

Alex nodded slowly, masking his displeasure with a tight smile. "That's wonderful," he said, his voice sounding strained.

Brigitte watched quietly as her husband undressed and joined her in bed. "You're upset, aren't you?"

"Don't be ridiculous. I'm very happy for you. Why would I be upset?" he answered his voice completely flat.

Brigitte sighed. "Alex, you're always so busy with your own career. I have to keep busy or else I'll just go crazy. As long as I can concentrate on my painting, I don't miss you as much. You understand, don't you?"

"Of course I do," he said and gave her a quick kiss on the cheek. Then he turned back, pulling the blankets over himself. "Good night, sweetheart," he said, abruptly ending any chance of continuing the discussion.

Brigitte answered with resignation. "Good night Alex."

• • • • •

Exactly one year after their move to New York, Alex finished the renovations on the last apartment in his building. A few weeks later, when the unit was rented, he burst into their apartment in the middle of the afternoon. "Tonight we celebrate," he told his stunned wife. "I'm taking you out to dinner at Lutèce."

Brigitte was ecstatic. This would be the first time she and Alex went out together for a romantic dinner. She changed into her prettiest dress, and to her delight, Alex noticed.

"You look beautiful tonight," he said as they walked into the famous restaurant.

Brigitte glowed. Maybe now that the renovations were behind them, Alex would finally have more time for her and David.

The dining room at Lutèce was crowded, but the Maitre'D quickly found them an unoccupied table. Alex ordered a bottle of champagne and when it arrived, he raised his glass. "To us. This is only the beginning, sweetheart. Someday I will have a hundred buildings like this one. I'll be making so much money; you won't even want to work anymore."

Brigitte's heart sank. Before she could answer, she felt a tap on her shoulder and turned. "Natalia!"

Natalia Berenson, covered in diamonds, smiled

down at them. "Brigitte, how lovely to see you! And this must be Alex. I am so happy to meet you at last. I was beginning to think you were a figment of Brigitte's imagination. Come, you must join us."

To refuse would have been impolite. "Nice to meet you too," said Alex, glowering as waiters rushed about, adding chairs and bringing plates and glasses to Natalia's table.

As soon as they were seated, Natalia made the introductions. "Alex, I'd like you to meet Gerald Masson. Brigitte, you two have already met."

Gerald Masson shook Alex's hand. "Brigitte," he said. "you look lovely as usual. Natalia tells me your paintings have been selling very well lately."

"Yes, they are." Brigitte answered flustered. After Natalia's party she had never mentioned Gerald Masson to her husband. There really had been nothing to tell. She turned nervously to Alex. "Gerald and I met at one of Natalia's parties. Actually, you two have something in common," she added. "Gerald is also in real estate."

"I'm also a great admirer of your wife's," added Gerald gallantly. "So you're in real estate too?"

Alex nodded. "Only in a very small way. I'm an

architect. I'm working on a residential development project at the moment. The only real estate I own is a building in Greenwich, a warehouse I transformed into modern loft apartments."

Gerald smiled politely. "Sounds interesting," he said.

Natalia jutted in. "Gerald is in the hotel business. He owns, how many is it now Gerald, sixteen hotels across the country?"

"Eighteen. I just opened a new hotel in L.A. and another one in Chicago."

Natalia continued, gushing. "You should see his Washington hotel. It's absolutely gorgeous. Oh, and by the way Brigitte, I spoke to DD earlier today and he mentioned that Josephine Livingston bought one of your paintings."

"Did she?" asked Brigitte overwhelmed. She turned to her husband. "Josephine has one of the best collections of modern art in the city."

Natalia continued. "It's a huge honor for any artist to have one of their paintings in Josephine's collection."

"That's wonderful," replied Alex, his expression contradicting his words.

As the evening progressed, Alex felt more and

more uncomfortable. Although Brigitte kept trying to include him into the conversation, it was painfully apparent to him that he knew none of the people and events they were talking about.

Brigitte has a whole life away from me. Tonight we were supposed to celebrate the completion of my project. Instead here we are, talking about her success.

He smiled tightly throughout the evening and waited impatiently for the evening to end. When the meal was finally over and people began making noises about leaving, Gerald pulled out his card and handed it. "If you ever want my help with some project, give me a call. I'm always looking for solid real estate investments."

"Thank you," said Alex. "I might take you up on that someday." Moments later, as the group was saying good bye, he could not help but notice that Gerald held Brigitte's hand a second too long.

On the way back home, he was fuming. "I don't ever want you to see that man again," he said to Brigitte.

"Alex, *pour l'amour de Dieu*, you're being unreasonable. I hardly know the man. I've only met him once. He's a friend of Natalia's."

"He was practically undressing you with his

eyes. It's damn clear he would like to be a lot more than your friend."

Brigitte was stunned. "Really Alex. You have nothing to worry about. Gerald lost his wife recently, and from what I hear, he is still mourning her. Besides," she continued gently. "I love you, remember?"

Alex was mollified. "Sorry. I guess I was just a bit jealous." He hesitated for a moment and continued. "I love you too."

The words brought tears to Brigitte's eyes. "Do you have any idea how long it's been since you told me?" she asked, her voice overcome with emotion.

To her joy, her husband reached over and held her hand gently. "I'll try to tell you more often," he promised.

That night, Alex made love to Brigitte more passionately than he had in a long time.

My dear God, Brigitte prayed silently later, still bathing in the afterglow of their lovemaking. Make this last. I've never been so happy. Please don't take this away from me.

The next morning, after Alex had left for work,

a large bouquet of red roses arrived at the door. Oh Alex! You're wonderful, thought Brigitte as she tore open the envelope. To her surprise, the card read simply, 'To a lovely lady', and it was signed, your friend, Gerald Masson.

Brigitte's disappointment was like a knife. She took the flowers to the kitchen and dumped them in the garbage before Alex could see them.

* * * * *

In the year since Andrew had hired him, Alex had seen the housing project grow from a flat, dusty piece of land to a row of fourteen attractive houses on groomed lawns. Although the houses were built inexpensively, they were beautifully and solid. But the model units had been open to the public for months, and although according to Andrew's projections, half of the project should have been sold by now, eleven were still available. It was a bitter disappointment for the young developer.

The dusty trailer was parked at the edge of the development project and was used as much as a sales office for potential customers, as it was as a drafting room and even, occasionally, as a kitchen and cafeteria for the construction workers. No matter how they tried to keep it looking neat, it was always a mess.

Alex was bending over the detail-sketch of a kitchen plan when Andrew McGregor walked in, slamming the door behind him. Alex looked up. "What's up?" he asked, surprised at his friend's scowling expression.

Andrew dug his hands into his pockets and cleared his throat. "I'm sorry, Alex. I don't know how to tell you this. The buyers who put the down payment on number five last week have changed their minds. They want their money back, and according to their purchase contract, I have no choice but to refund them." He sighed. "Which means I won't be able to pay you this week."

Alex leaned back in his chair in shock and waited for Andrew to explain, which he did feverishly. "It's only temporary, of course. I wish I could go to my father for more money, but I can't. The last time I did, he made it clear that he won't lend me another dime. But I have a few other prospects that are just about to sign. As soon as I get some money, you'll be the first to be paid."

Alex groaned as he calculated quickly. The

income from his apartment building would cover his mortgage and living expenses. Going without a paycheck temporarily would not cause him any hardship. However, Andrew didn't have to know this. Suddenly an idea came to him. "I have a proposition for you," he said, crossing his arms.

Andrew looked up, hesitantly. "Shoot."

Alex thought for a moment on how to best approach this. "I want to buy another building," he said, as the details began to fall into place in his mind. "I want to convert it, just as I did the one I live in. Instead of paying me a salary, I would like you to cosign the loan at the bank. You wouldn't have to put out any money for it, and in the meantime, you wouldn't have to pay me any salary."

"How much do you need?"

Alex told him.

Andrew gasped. "But I would have to put up my own project as collateral. You're asking me to risk everything I've worked for!"

"You're already in trouble, and we both know it. The houses are not selling fast enough. You still need me, and unless I'm wrong, I don't think you can afford to pay me at all anymore. You've already cut the construction crew down to the bare minimum. This way, you can finish your project without having to keep paying me. What could be better?"

Andrew thought furiously. He was in a bind and as much as he hated to admit it, Alex had sized up the situation perfectly. "Let me think about it," he said and stormed out of the trailer.

For the next few days, Alex continued showing up for work at seven o'clock sharp every morning. One week later, Andrew walked into the trailer and pulled up a chair. "I've been giving some thought to your idea. It's not bad," he admitted grudgingly. "But I want to see the building. I'll agree to your proposal if you can satisfy me that your plan is sound."

That evening, Alex went home early. Brigitte was on the telephone but she ended the conversation as soon as she saw him. "Alex, what a surprise," she said, hanging up. "I didn't expect you home so early."

"Who was that?" he asked, suddenly suspicious.

She hesitated. "Gerald Masson," she answered apologetically. She tried to explain. "He just called to tell me he bought one of my paintings."

Alex stared at her blandly; then he turned and walked back out.

* * * * *

CHAPTER 5

Gerald Masson knew it had been a mistake to call her the moment Brigitte mumbled her excuse. He stared at the telephone on his office desk, berating himself. *You are a fool. Brigitte is not only married, but very much in love with her husband. What do you imagine can come of this? Nothing!* He remembered her reaction when she recognized his voice. There wasn't just a surprise; there was something else, a slight strain in her greeting. Brigitte had no feelings for him other than friendship. *And if I keep pursuing her, she won't even feel even that.*

· · · · ·

Alex had been driving aimlessly for over an hour, when he noticed the 'for sale' sign on an old abandoned building. Something about it reminded him of his own building, before the renovations. *If the price is good, this one might be interesting.* He took down the name and telephone number of the real-estate agent and drove back home. He slipped quietly into the apartment and climbed into bed without saying a word.

The next day he called the agent. "You have a good eye," the woman told him on the telephone. She sounded knowledgeable and friendly. "The building is older but solid. It was built in the nineteen twenties and was one of the first buildings with an underground parking garage, which makes it ideal for developing into a residential project. Whoever picks it up will have a great deal. This used to be a bakery until a few years ago. The business was bought up by an international chain. They've since moved to more modern facilities, and the owner wants to unload it fast." She quoted the price and made an appointment to show him the property later that afternoon.

They met in front of the building. When Alex climbed out of his car, Susan Temple was already waiting. The agent was in her late twenties, with a shapely figure, long blond hair and deep blue eyes.

"I-I'm sorry I'm late," he said. "My meeting went on longer than I'd anticipated." He had not expected the real estate agent to be so attractive.

Susan Temple watched his reaction with amusement. "I hope it was successful," she said graciously. She held out her hand. "Nice to meet you, Mr. Ivanov."

"Yes, it was successful, thank you," he said shaking her hand. "It's nice to meet you too. And please call me Alex."

"All right, Alex. How about if I show you inside?"

She walked him through the building, pointing out the highlights along the way. "There are over one hundred thousand square feet of space, distributed on four floors, not counting the underground garage where the bakery trucks used to park." They continued a little further. "Notice the old wooden columns. Those go for a fortune in antique stores, but, if I were you, I'd keep them. They add a lot of character to the place." In the basement, she showed him through the boiler room and the electrical room. "Everything is solid. This building has been here nearly fifty years and there's no reason it shouldn't stand here another hundred."

Alex looked around, as he evaluated possibilities. *I could easily get forty apartments out of this building*, he thought.

Almost as if she could read his mind, Susan Temple said, "And even if you end up with only thirty or forty apartments, you would make back your investment in no time."

"That depends on how much the renovations will cost."

"You won't have to do anything structurally. The owner had a building engineer's report done. The structure is solid. You would have to separate the space into apartments, put in plumbing and update the electrical of course, but other than that, most of the work would be mainly cosmetic."

Alex was impressed with her quick assessment of the situation. When they got back to the main entrance, Alex heard himself ask. "Would you join me for dinner? I'd like to go over a few of the details."

Susan smiled. "I'd be happy to help in any way I can."

Alex took her to a quiet, out of the way restaurant with small, intimate tables. Music played softly in the background.

"We are here to talk about business, right?" asked Susan with a playful smile. She was aware of the attraction Alex felt for her and was surprised at how much she wanted to respond. *He is a very attractive man*, she thought, her eyes taking in the thick black hair, the strong square jaw and the wide shoulders.

"Unless you prefer talking about something else?" said Alex. He was enjoying himself. It had been a long time since he had flirted with a beautiful woman.

The rest of the evening they talked about everything except business. To his delight, Alex found that she was more than just beautiful. She was intelligent. She had a sense of humor and she was genuinely interested in him. Sparks flew.

Toward the end of the meal, the conversation became more businesslike. "So, is that what you want to do? Turn the building into residential apartments?" she asked.

"I'd like to turn it into a co-op. I think the time is ripe for a project of this kind in Greenwich."

"I think that's a wonderful idea. A few developers are experimenting with the concept of co-ops and they seem to be very successful. Greenwich would be a great location for a project of that kind."

At the end of the evening, when he walked Susan back to her car, Alex wished he could see her again. *What am I doing?* He reprimanded himself, feeling a twinge of guilt. It had been no accident that he had not once mentioned his wife during the entire evening.

* * * * *

The next day he showed Andrew the building, outlining his ideas for the project. Andrew had endless question. "What about permits?'

"No problem. The real estate agent assures me that the area allows residential zoning."

"What if the construction takes longer than you think?"

"I've gone over the figures and even if we take six months more, we can still cover the mortgage payments."

"Parking in this area is difficult. Where do you expect the tenants to park their cars?"

"The building has an underground garage. I've checked, and it's almost large enough for two cars per unit."

To every one of Andrew's objections, Alex had a prepared answer. "I see you've really thought this over," admitted Andrew finally. Alex held his breath. Andrew paused for a moment. "I guess you've made it impossible for me to refuse."

A few weeks later, Andrew cosigned the loan, and Alex closed the deal.

Susan Temple was at the signing. "I guess you won't need me anymore," she said as they shook hands afterwards. She sounded disappointed.

"I'm sure we'll run into each other again," replied Alex.

Susan Temple watched him walk away. *I'll make sure of that, Alex Ivanov.*

Alex worked night and day, drawing the plans. Two weeks later, he submitted them to the city permit department, slipping a one hundred dollar bill to the clerk. One month later, the renovations on the building began. Crews worked night and day in an effort to complete the project in record time, and within months the model suite was ready to show.

Alex had huge billboards erected, advertising large and luxurious co-ops for sale. He rented a trailer and had the interior decorated with deep pile carpets and rich, comfortable couches. On the walls he displayed floor plans of the different apartments. Then he called Susan Temple.

"I need a sales team and I'd like you to be in charge of it."

Susan tried to keep her voice steady, but she was out of breath. Since the day she had first laid eyes on Alex Ivanov, she had been unable to keep him out of her mind. "What kind of a salary are we talking about?" she asked, attempting to disguise her delight by focusing on business.

"I was thinking of putting you on a four-per-cent commission. The projected sales are one million dollars. If you sell every unit, you will make forty thousand dollars." It was a fortune and he knew it, but professionally and otherwise, Susan Temple was worth every penny of it.

"I want five per cent."

"What?"

"In a bad year I make nearly double that amount. I'm the number-one real-estate agent in my office. I can guarantee I'll sell every one of your apartments in less than six months, but I want five per cent commission, and I'll work for you afternoons and evenings. Mornings are mine. Take it or leave it."

Alex laughed. "You're pretty sure of yourself, aren't you?"

"Mr. Ivanov, your project needs me more than I need it."

Alex hesitated. "You drive a hard bargain Miss Temple."

She could not contain her joy any longer and burst into laughter. "I'll take that as a yes. When do I start?"

Her first day at work, one week later, Susan Temple was sitting at the elegant secretary in a corner of the trailer when the phone rang. She picked it up and answered in her usual pleasant voice. "Sales office, may I help you?"

"Hello, this is Mrs. Ivanov speaking. May I speak to Mr. Ivanov please?"

Susan heard the words through a roaring in her ears. She thought she might faint and had to grab the desk for support. Somehow, she heard herself answer pleasantly. "One moment Mrs. Ivanov, I'll see if he's here."

She went out to the entrance of the building and found Alex talking to some contractors. "Alex, your wife is on the telephone for you." She was proud of her composure. *He must have no idea of how I feel.*

"Tell her I'll be right there." He spoke a few words to the men then hurried toward the trailer.

Susan Temple did not sleep that night. She hugged her pillow and screamed her frustration into it. She could not believe the unfairness of it all. For the first time in years, she had met a man she could love. It had never occurred to her that he might be married. *I'll just have to put him out of my mind. I will meet somebody else someday. Alex Ivanov is not the only man in the world.* But she did not believe that for one second.

* * * * *

Months had passed since the start of the project. Alex was in a dilemma. He still had his contract with Andrew to fulfill, and with his own new development underway, there weren't enough hours in the day to accomplish everything that needed to be done. If he neglected Andrew's project, his friend stood to lose his housing development. If he neglected his own, his sales projections would not be met in time to make his payments, and then Andrew's project would be taken over by the bank to cover the loan he had cosigned. One way or another, Andrew would end up being the loser. *There's only one solution. I have to put all my energies into my own project.*

In Andrew's office the next day, Alex tried to explain the situation.

Andrew listened, as drops of moisture broke out on his forehead. He was livid. "Your first obligation is to me. You knew when you bought that building that you still had to honor your contractual obligations to me. You would never have been able to buy that building if it wasn't for me. And now you stab me in the back like that?"

Alex shook his head. "You're not listening to what I'm telling you. The way I look at it, you stand to lose less if I complete this project. Don't forget, you cosigned the loan. If I go under, you will too."

Andrew was shaken to his core as the reality of the situation hit him. He stared stonily at his friend. "You bastard. You swore to me that cosigning would not put me at the slightest risk, and now I find out I could lose my entire project," he sputtered angrily.

"I don't know what to say Andrew, except that I'm sorry. If you'll only try to see it..."

Andrew stood up slowly. His legs were shaking. "Trusting you was the biggest mistake of my life," he said, his voice rasping. He walked out of the trailer, leaving the door swinging open behind him. Alex waited for a few minutes, and then closed the door softly.

* * * * *

In the days that followed, Alex tried to find some other solution to the problem. He called the bank and pleaded for an extension on his loan, only to be told that unless he made his payment on time, the bank would start immediate foreclosure proceedings. That night he went to a bar and got roaring drunk.

The next morning when he woke up, he had no idea where he was.

"Good morning. How are you feeling?" It was Susan Temple's voice.

He turned his head and felt as though a sledgehammer was pounding on it. There were two Susans standing before him. "Where am I?" he asked. His mouth felt like sandpaper.

"You're in my apartment." Susan leaned over

and put her hand on his forehead. "I think you'll survive."

"How-how did I get here?"

Susan hesitated. "You called me in the middle of the night and begged me to let you come over." She trailed a lazy finger along the outline of his mouth, and gave him a suggestive smile. "You said you loved me, remember?"

He tried to think. He vaguely remembered the bar, countless double Scotches. He saw his clothes neatly folded on a chair. "Did... did we..."

"Did we make love?" There was amusement in her voice.

He waited, dreading the answer.

"You mean to say you don't remember? And you told me I was the best you ever had."

He thought of Brigitte suddenly. "My wife..."

"Don't worry. I have a friend who owed me a favor. He called your wife last night. He told her you had a bit too much to drink and would spend the night at his place. She was very understanding."

Alex's eyes were slowly focusing. Slowly, he realized that Susan Temple was naked. His eyes roved over her hungrily. Damn, she was beautiful.

Susan pulled the sheet off Alex and looked down at his erection. "Well, well. And what have we here?" she said huskily. "I see you're feeling much better indeed."

* * * * *

Brigitte was in her studio, painting. She heard the front door open and a moment later Alex appeared, looking disheveled. She put down her paint brush. "Do you want a cup of coffee?" she asked. She was doing her best to stay calm.

"No. I'll just go and take a shower."

"Alex!" He turned around. "Alex. Is there something we should talk about?"

He shrugged, and gave her an innocent look. "Not as far as I know. I'm just going to take a shower. I won't be long."

Brigitte watched her husband walk away and suddenly felt cold. She shivered. *What is wrong with me? So he went out and got a bit drunk last night. With the problems he has, it's a wonder he's holding up this well.* But somewhere deep inside, she knew there was another problem, one she had no idea how she should handle.

Alex stood under the hot spay, but the shower did nothing to wash away his guilt. If anything it only made him feel worse. The water helped clear his mind, and now he realized the extent of his betrayal. He stepped out of the stall and toweled himself briskly. *What if Brigitte found out somehow? Where had he put Susan's telephone number?* He riffled through his wallet with guilty paranoia when he suddenly came across Gerald Masson's business card. He pulled it out and stared at it as scenes from the evening at Lutèce flashed through his mind. *That arrogant bastard*, he thought and threw it into the waste basket. Then, an idea dawned on him. He fished the card back out and stared at it.

• • • • •

At the prearranged breakfast meeting the following Friday, Gerald Masson sipped his coffee and studied Alex as he sat across from him. *He's nervous*, he thought as he noted the forced smile, the tightness in the younger man's voice. *I wonder what he wants from me.*

Alex talked on. "This is the coldest August that I remember in years. I bet the leaves will be turning red by the end of the—"

"I'm sure you didn't ask for a meeting with me to discuss the weather," Gerald interrupted suddenly.

Alex stopped in midsentence. "No. You're right." He pulled a stack of papers from his briefcase and set them on the table. "You told me you were always looking for solid for real-estate investments. I've decided to let you take a look at these."

Gerald listened as Alex explained the projects, showing plans and projections, and then he said, "Wait a minute." He leaned forward and stared Alex in the eye. "You're telling me that both projects are gold mines, but if they are as good as you say, what the hell do you need me for?" He leaned back against his chair again, drumming his fingers on the table. "Why don't you tell me the whole story? You know I'll find out sooner or later. If you want me to do business with you, you had better tell me yourself."

Alex smiled and spread his hands open in a helpless gesture. "There's only one thing we don't have. Unless we can come up with enough working capital to tide us over the next few months, the banks will foreclose." Even now, as he admitted to his precarious position, Alex's whole attitude was one of confidence.

The guy's got nerves of steel. Gerald lifted an eyebrow. "How much?"

"One quarter of a million dollars."

Gerald let out a low whistle. "Doesn't sound like such a great deal to me."

Alex shook his head. "But in reality, it won't cost you a dime. All we need is your guarantee as financial backer."

"If I understand correctly, that's the offer you made McGregor, and look at the position he's in now."

"There's one big difference between McGregor and you. McGregor sank everything he had into his project. If he loses, he loses everything. You, on the other hand, will lose nothing. The worse that could happen to you is that you could be forced to take over both our projects. And that," concluded Alex, "would mean even greater profits for you in the long run."

Gerald thought quickly. All he could think about was Brigitte. *She reminds me so much of Kate*, he thought sadly. *If her husband's projects go belly up, what will happen to her?* He was almost tempted to let this brash young man sink on the chance that bankruptcy might make Brigitte leave him. But even as the thought crossed his mind, he knew she was the loyal type, and would stand by her husband even if it meant hardship for her. He chased the thought from his mind and tried to concentrate on what Alex was saying.

"I wouldn't have come to you if the problem was mine alone," Alex was saying. "But, Andrew McGregor stands to lose the most," repeated Alex.

"I understand." Gerald's mind kept working furiously. He wished there was some way he could come to the aid of Brigitte without committing himself financially to her husband. But to let him down, was to let her down, and that was as impossible as it would have been to refuse Kate.

By the time Alex finished outlining his proposal Gerald had made up his mind.

"OK," he said with a curt nod. "Now let's just hope McGregor cooperates."

* * * * *

Chapter 6

Later that evening Gerald stopped by Natalia's. He found the heavy actress in her sunroom, lying on her taffeta sofa with her Abyssinian cat on her lap and a plate of chocolate-covered cherries on the occasional table at hand's reach.

"Have a cherry," Natalia offered.

"No thanks," he said, and mixed himself a drink at the bar while Natalia set the plate back down, taking a handful of the chocolates. She ate quietly as she listened to Gerald's account of the meeting. She shook her head in amazement when he told her of his decision.

"Let me get this straight. You agreed to back Alex Ivanov because his wife reminds you of Kate?"

"Don't be ridiculous," replied Gerald vehemently and took another swig of his gin and tonic. "One thing has nothing to do with the other. Alex's project is sound."

Natalia leaned back on her sofa and studied her friend closely as he fiddled nervously with his drink and avoided her gaze. "You may be able to fool yourself, Gerald Masson, but don't imagine for one minute that you are fooling me. You are in love with Brigitte aren't you?"

Gerald's eyebrows shot up. "In love with...? Really, Natalia, sometimes you surprise even me with your silly ideas."

You protest too much, thought Natalia as she watched her friend take another long swallow.

* * * * *

Four days later, in the prestigious offices of Maxwell, Maxwell and Hawthorn, attorneys at law, all the legal papers pertaining to the deal were duly signed and notarized. Anthony Maxwell senior handed each of the three men their copy of the agreement. Maxwell explained. "As of this moment, you are partners. Mr. Ivanov, you own fifty one per cent of the company. The remaining shares are divided equally between Mr. McGregor and Mr. Masson." He smiled benignly and continued. "May your new company prosper." Almost as an afterthought, he asked, "What have you decided to call your company?"

For a moment nobody spoke. They had been too busy, working out the details of the deal, to even begin thinking about what to name the newly formed company.

"Power Properties," said Alex suddenly. The name had just popped into his mind.

Maxwell nodded. "Good name."

"When it comes to power," added Alex, "a company can never have too much."

* * * * *

Later that evening, as the three new partners walked out of the bar of The Pierre Hotel where they had been quietly celebrating, a pretty blonde woman at a table near the entrance, turned sharply and watched them leave.

"What's the matter babe?" her drunken

companion asked sullenly. "You see someone you'd rather be with than me?"

"You are so cute when you're jealous," answered Anne Turner sweetly as she gave her companion's thigh a squeeze under the tablecloth. "Just someone I thought I recognized. I was wrong. The guy I knew wouldn't have the bucks to get into a place like this." She stuck out her bottom lip in a petulant pout and leaned closer to him. "Come on, baby, tell me you love me."

Her partner hesitated. He was aware of her hand massaging his thigh and felt himself becoming aroused. He was totally helpless when it came to the beautiful blonde. The things that woman could do with her hands and her mouth were enough to drive any man insane. He took a deep breath. "You know I'm crazy about you, Anne."

Anne Turner laughed. "You really are, aren't you?" He nodded. "So what are going to do about it?" she asked suddenly serious.

"W-what do you mean?"

She shrugged. "It seems very simple to me. I love you. You love me. Like the song goes, 'Love and marriage, baby, they go together like a horse and carriage.'"

From the look in her eyes, he knew she was serious. Suddenly he felt her hand move up to his crotch.

"Don't you agree?" she asked. Meanwhile, her fingers found the zipper and tugged. He moaned. "So when do you think we should do it?" She smiled, slipping her hand into his shorts.

He tried to say no, but couldn't. He nodded weakly. "You got me by the balls, babe."

• • • • •

Chapter 7

According to the terms of the agreement, Andrew McGregor's housing project became a part of Power Properties, of which Alex Ivanov was president. The way Alex looked at it, he had done nothing wrong. He had saved Andrew from certain disaster. And as for Gerald Masson, whatever investment the man had made into the company would be repaid tenfold. He was convinced that Power Properties would someday be a major real estate company. In fact, as far as he was concerned, he had done both men a favor, and he walked around with his chest out. It was a situation the two vice-presidents resented but had no choice but tolerate. After all, they had agreed to his terms.

Alex embraced his role of leader with

enthusiasm. Every day he arrived at work filled with ideas. In exchange for free advertising, he made arrangements with a prestigious furniture store to decorate the model suite of both the newly renovated apartment building and the now completed housing project. Next, he approached a financing company and convinced them to give the buyers of his co-ops a reduced mortgage rate. In return the lenders were guaranteed all of Power Properties' business. Following this he bought a full-page advertisement in the *New York Times* and offered rebates on all units sold before the end of the month. Sales soared.

He worked incessantly, coordinating the schedule of construction crews so that every step of the project was completed quickly. "Time is money," he repeated constantly. Behind his back workers nudged each other and rolled their eyes every time they heard those words.

His ideas, which originally had been met with resistance by his partners, proved to be brilliant, and soon both Andrew's housing and the co-op project were sold out. Andrew and Gerald had no choice but to grudgingly admit that Alex Ivanov knew what he was doing, and that maybe, just maybe, the deal Alex Ivanov had rammed down their throats would work out to their advantage.

The Sting of the Scorpio

Gerald also watched and waited in silence as Alex continued his flagrant affair. Surely Brigitte would find out, and when she did, that would be the end of the marriage. Wouldn't it?

* * * * *

Susan Temple looked out from the window of the trailer at the finished co-op building. She had just sold the last unit of the project, but although she had fulfilled her contract and was fifty thousand dollars richer, she was now without a job. She feared she might also be without a lover.

In the ten months since the start of her affair with Alex, she had fallen madly in love with him. She had initially hoped that he would leave his wife and marry her, but as time went by and Alex made no mention of that possibility, she knew that her dream had little chance of becoming reality. She also knew that any effort on her part to force Alex to choose between Brigitte and her, would only drive him away.

When she first began to work for Alex she had done everything humanly possible to make him love her. But to no avail. One night, depressed and angry at the world, she had gone to a bar with the intention of getting herself piss drunk. With any luck, that might give her at least one good night's sleep.

To her immense surprise, the first person she saw when she got there, was Alex. He was sitting at the bar, gulping down one Scotch after another. Not one to stand by idly, Susan decided to give Fate a hand, and many double Scotches later, when Alex finally stumbled out of the bar, she offered him a ride.

She helped him in the car and drove him to her apartment where he immediately passed out. The next morning when she realized that he remembered nothing of the previous evening, she knew that once again, luck had been on her side.

"And you said I was the best you ever had," she told him, standing naked before him. She watched his eyes change from disbelief to lust.

That had been the beginning of the affair. She closed her eyes and stifled a sob as a wave of almost unbearable sorrow shot through her body.

From then on, they had been lovers. And for a time, that had been enough, but no longer. Every time Alex made love to her, only to rush out minutes later, leaving her feeling miserable, she died a little more inside. It was a situation she couldn't tolerate one minute longer. Yet the thought of ending the relationship made her feel even worse. *I'm so stupid. I should have known he'd never leave his wife*, she thought and the sharp pain came back. *But I can't live without him. I've got to find a way. If only his wife would leave him.*

Once the idea began to form, she couldn't put it out of her mind. For a long time, she stood there, thinking. Then she turned away from the window, gathered her courage, and picked up the telephone.

* * * * *

In her studio, Brigitte put the telephone back in its cradle and looked at Réjeanne. "That's strange," she said. "Alex never mentioned any celebration."

"It seems to me that Alex doesn't mention much of anything lately, or am I wrong?" said Réjeanne as she set the cup of coffee on the table next to the easel.

"Oh Réjeanne, you shouldn't criticize him. You know the poor man is just busy. He has so many things to worry about."

"He should spend more time at home, if you

ask me. He comes in at all hours of the night and if, by some grace of God he is here, he's preoccupied. He never spends any time with you and David."

"Now that the projects are over, things will change, you'll see. That was his sales manager on the phone. They're having a small celebration at the office later tonight. He wants me to come. So you see, he does think about me doesn't he?"

"He didn't even call you himself."

"Réjeanne! What's wrong with you? I thought you liked Alex."

"I do like him. But ever since you've started painting again, he's changed. I think he doesn't like that you're pursuing your own career."

Brigitte struggled to keep her smile from slipping. Réjeanne was right, and she knew it. "I was already a successful artist in Paris when he met me. He can't expect me to give up everything."

Réjeanne shook her head. "No man wants to share his wife with her career. Have you ever thought of that?"

Brigitte nodded. "Yes. I have. But what can I do? David is at school all day. Alex is busy running his company, and you take care of the apartment. Nobody needs me. I love painting. If I don't paint, I'll go crazy."

Réjeanne was thoughtful for a moment. "What would you do if you had to choose between your marriage and your career."

Brigitte couldn't bring herself to answer.

Later that evening, Brigitte applied her makeup meticulously and slipped into a new dress. *Alex loves me. I just have to be more attentive to him.* She climbed into a cab and gave the directions to the co-op project. Twenty minutes later, she stepped out and headed for the trailer. *That's strange. All the lights are out.*

At the door of the trailer, she stopped for a second. She could hear movement inside, and something that sounded like moaning. *Mon Dieu, someone is hurt.* She pulled the door open and walked in. In the dim light, she could see two bodies intertwined on the couch. The way they were moving left no doubt to her imagination. *What...* Her hand flew to her mouth, strangling the cry in her throat. She turned and ran.

At that moment Alex looked up and saw his wife rush out the door. "Wait! I can explain. Brigitte, please don't go! Brigitte!"

"Let her go," said Susan. "She was bound to find out about us someday. It might as well be now."

"You don't know what you're saying." He dressed as fast as he could and ran after Brigitte.

• • • • •

Real despair did not hit Brigitte until she got home. She sat in her darkened bedroom, trying to understand what she had done wrong.

If only she had not resumed her painting again.

If only she had spent more time with Alex.

If only she had known what to do when he began drifting away from her.

If only... And now it was too late. *Everyone I have ever loved has betrayed me. I wish I were dead.*

• • • • •

When Alex arrived, the bedroom door was locked. He knocked. "Brigitte. Please, I have to talk to you." There was no answer. He had never imagined that he could feel so miserable.

The next morning, Alex did not go to work. Brigitte came out of her bedroom, her back straight and her head high. Alex followed her to her studio, pleading. "Please Brigitte, let's talk about this."

I will not let him see how much he's hurt me. She picked up her brush and began to paint. "What is there to talk about? You're having an affair. It's not the end of the world."

Her reaction was not what he had expected. Tears, certainly anger, but not this coldness. "So you won't leave me?"

"Why would I want to do that?"

Relief washed over him. He had been given a reprieve. "Thank God. I don't know what I would have done if you'd left me." He took her in his arms and buried his face in her hair. "I love you. And I promise I'll never hurt you again."

Later, Brigitte remembered how she had wanted to cringe when he touched her. The memory of what she had seen in the trailer was stamped indelibly on her mind.

● ● ● ● ●

Natalia Berenson's brownstone was a stone's throw from central park. She sat on her silk taffeta sofa, surrounded by dozens of satin and velvet, beaded pillows. Her heavily made-up eyes were inscrutable as they stared at the multitude of silver framed pictures on the baby grand piano across the room.

Brigitte sat before her, nervously trying to explain her decision. "The only way I can make it work is by devoting myself entirely to being Alex's wife. I cannot balance a career and still give one hundred per cent to my marriage. It is just not possible." She ventured a glance at Natalia. "I know how much you wanted me to succeed. You were so kind, introducing me to so many influential people, helping me find an agent. I just hope you are not angry with me."

Natalia softened. She shook her head, sending her many chins quivering. "Angry? No, I'm not angry. I'm disappointed. That's not the same thing. I've been married myself, a number of times as you know, and having my own career and interests has always been a great satisfaction in my life. Husbands can come and go but a career is yours as long as you want it. Brigitte, you are very talented. You have as much to contribute to this world as Alex does. I don't think leaving your career will in any way improve your marriage." A sudden suspicion came to her mind. "Did Alex ask you to do this?"

"Alex has nothing to do with this. He didn't even know I was considering doing this."

Natalia studied Brigitte. She noticed the circles under her eyes, the resignation and sadness in her smile. "Then for God's sake, why?"

Brigitte could not begin to explain how, now that she had finally allowed herself to love, her desire to be loved in return was the single most desperate need in her life. She looked down at her hands. "This is what I have to do."

* * * * *

Gerald Masson's reaction was stronger. As soon as he heard, he drove over to the Ivanov residence and confronted Brigitte. "Is it true? Natalia just told me you want to stop painting."

Brigitte invited him in and he sat at one end of the white vinyl-covered sofa.

"Would you like a glass of wine?" she said, trying to delay the conversation she knew would come. She disappeared and returned a moment later with a glass of Cabernet which she handed to him, avoiding his eyes.

"Tell me it's not true, Brigitte," he repeated.

She sighed, and said, "I can't give one hundred per cent of myself to a career, to being a mother and a wife. I simply sorted out my priorities."

Gerald looked at her, sitting stiffly on the sofa, looking resigned. "Brigitte, your talent is a gift. You can't ignore it. I know you. Painting is oxygen to your soul. You mustn't give it up."

"What I decide to do is my business. I don't see how it affects you."

Gerald's voice softened. "It affects me Brigitte, because I care for you." As he spoke, he moved closer to her and almost against his will, his hand lifted up to caress her cheek. "Haven't you guessed by now the way I feel about you? I only want to see you happy. And I know that if you stop painting you will be very unhappy."

Brigitte pulled away, trembling. When she spoke, her voice was strained. "That's very sweet of you. Of course I care for you too. You are a very dear friend." She forced herself to smile and patted his hand affectionately. "But this is a decision I've made for my husband and for our marriage." The meaning could not have been any clearer.

Long after he had left, Brigitte remained shaken. Why did she feel such turmoil every time she saw him? If only Alex could be more like... *How can I even think that way?* she reprimanded herself guiltily. *I love Alex for the man he is. He doesn't have to change in any way. He is my husband.*

* * * * *

Although she made a sincere effort to put the discovery of Alex's infidelity behind her, Brigitte found it impossible to forget. Even when Alex swore to her that he had ended the affair with Susan Temple, Brigitte kept her distance. In bed one night, Alex listened to Brigitte's breathing and snuggled close to her. "Are you sleeping, sweetheart?"

Brigitte stirred but did not answer. Alex tried again. "Brigitte?" His hand traveled slowly to her breasts. He felt her body stiffen. He rolled over to his back and sighed with exasperation. "How long are you planning to keep punishing me?" he asked.

There was a short silence before Brigitte stirred and answered. "I'm not punishing you," she replied. "I'm doing the best I can."

Alex's voice rose sharply. "You're not doing a

thing. It's been weeks and you still won't let me anywhere near you. How long is this supposed to go on?"

"I-I don't know." And suddenly the tears she had held back for so long came pouring out. She felt Alex's arms wrap themselves around her as he whispered sweet words in her ears. The pleasure was so intense; it drowned out the misery of the last few weeks. "I love you," he whispered. "Don't you know you're the only woman I've ever loved?" The words were like balm to her shattered soul.

"And I love you," she replied through her tears. Suddenly her body was on fire. She wanted him, needed him with a passion she had never experienced. When Alex entered her, her pleasure was so intense; she exploded in waves of ecstasy.

Afterwards, as they lay in each other's arms, Brigitte told him of her decision to stop painting.

"I want to be a real wife to you," she said. "I want to cook for you. I want to iron your shirts. I want to ..."

Alex covered her mouth gently with a finger. "Stop. This is too much. I admit I wasn't thrilled that you went back to painting, but you don't have to cook for me. Réjeanne's cooking is fine."

Brigitte laughed. "What? You don't trust my cooking?"

"I plan to keep you so busy in the bedroom; you won't have time for anything else."

As she drifted off to sleep, Brigitte thought she had never heard such beautiful words. *I made the right decision. Abandoning my career is a small price to pay for a happy marriage. I'll devote myself entirely to him, and everything will be all right.*

* * * * *

Over the next five years the relatively new field of co-op properties witnessed an incredible growth. At the forefront of this movement was Power Properties. During that period, Power Properties bought, renovated, and sold buildings at a dizzying rate. The company's success was more than even Alex had ever anticipated.

"Didn't I tell you I'd make so much money, you'd never want to work again?" asked Alex to Brigitte one night. It was their wedding anniversary and they were enjoying a rare evening alone.

Brigitte smiled. "I never doubted for a moment that you would become successful."

"You know," said Alex thoughtfully. "I think it might be a good idea for us to be more visible. We should start working on becoming more socially prominent. Why don't we ever have people over? We can't expect to get invited anywhere unless we do so inviting too."

Brigitte hesitated. *An occasional evening is the only time alone I have with my husband. If we start entertaining, I won't even have those anymore.* But all she said was, "If that's what you want."

Alex was ebullient. "I think it's a great idea. Do you have any idea how many deals are made over dinner tables?"

The next morning, Brigitte called Natalia. "Natalia, I was thinking of giving a small dinner party. Do you think you could help me make up a guest list?"

Although, their first dinner party was no more than a dress rehearsal, as Alex called it, the guest list was short but impressive. There was Burt Holmsby the owner of Holmsby Hotels, his wife Tricia who was mentioned in the society columns almost as regularly as the newly married Jackie Onassis. Also present was Donald Richardson who had made a name for himself as the promoter of a number of sports figures. His wife was Betty Moore, the star on one of the popular daytime soaps.

"Small and intimate," specified Alex. "After all, this is our first effort. We don't want to start off with too big an affair."

Brigitte decorated the dining room into something out One Thousand and One Nights. She covered the table with a gold lamé cloth. For a centerpiece, she used a dried flower arrangement which she had spray painted gold. The gold platted cutlery, borrowed from Natalia, and the crystal—purchased at Sotheby's for just this occasion—sparkled in the dimmed lights. For the occasion, she planned to serve seafood fettuccini sprinkled with caviar, and for desert, a spectacular *Mousse au cognac flambé*.

"You did well," said Alex after the last guests had left. He lay naked on the bed, a towel covering his groin. "But you know, I don't think serving pasta was a good idea."

"Why not," asked Brigitte. "Everybody loved it."

"Of course. Don't get me wrong. It was very good. It's just that... pasta, for God's sake. Can't you think of something more imaginative? After all, we were trying to impress those people."

Brigitte did not reply. *Why do we have to impress anyone?*

"And I think we should start looking for a proper house. I was embarrassed to invite those people here."

"Alex, our apartment was featured in City and Country Homes. Everyone loves it."

"That was fine while I was still making a name for myself. But now, it's time to live like the rich folks, because sweetheart, that's what we are, rich folks." He laughed. "Tomorrow, I want you to start looking for a new house. I want it big, and impressive."

Brigitte looked around the room which she had decorated with so much love when she first arrived in New York. *I'll miss this place.* "I'll call the real estate company tomorrow," she said.

• • • • •

The president of Power Properties and his vice-presidents were gathered around the conference table of their luxurious new headquarters. Alex picked up the last quarterly financial report and handed copies to Gerald and Andrew. He waited for them to study the figures. "I think we're ready to diversify," he said as soon as the last sheet had been put down.

Gerald looked up from his brief. "What have you got in mind?"

Alex opened his folder and pulled out a stack of pictures. "Take a look at this." He handed them out, leaned back and watched their reactions.

Andrew quickly flipped through the pictures and looked at Alex, puzzled. "These are shots of the old Grand Palace. The place is a dump. The city wants to tear it down and build a new hotel on that spot. What would Power Properties want with a dump like that?"

Alex smiled, arrogantly. "What's the matter with you? Don't you have any vision, Andrew? For over half a century, the Grand Palace was the most prestigious hotel in the city. Even now, decades after the place has lost its reputation, the name is still recognized all over the world. The Grand Palace is a landmark. People will always remember the balls that were held there, the stars who stayed there, the glamour of the place. I don't want it to be torn down. I want to buy it so that Power Properties can restore it to the old luxury hotel that it used to be. And that, my friends, will make Power Properties a household name."

Gerald looked at Andrew and shrugged. "You know he won't give us a moment's peace until we agree to it, don't you?"

• • • • •

When Alex approached the mayor and made his proposal, the man laughed. "Just because you were successful in renovating a few old buildings into co-ops doesn't mean you can handle a project this size. Even if we wanted to restore the Grand Palace, which we don't, we would give it to an established firm, not to some newcomer like Power Properties. Now if you'll excuse me, I have some business to attend to."

Alex was more determined than ever. "What we have to do," he told his vice-presidents later, "is drown city hall with petitions to save the hotel. The Grand Palace is not just a landmark. It's a piece of New York's history. It's a part of every New Yorker's heritage. It would be a crime to tear it down. As far as I'm concerned, the mayor is a fool. He's just an old man without vision."

Gerald Masson sat quietly during Alex's tirade against the mayor. At the end he said, "What we need is someone with a lot of influence to gather support for us." He paused for a second before continuing. "We need Natalia Berenson."

"Why didn't I think of that?" asked Alex. "Okay, Gerald, whatever it takes, you get her to come work for us."

* * * * *

When Gerald approached Natalia, she listened to his offer in silence, petting the cat on her lap. For all her calm outward appearance, she had never thought faster in her life. Since her divorce from number seven as she always referred to her last husband, she managed to live a comfortable life, selling off her famous jewelry one piece at a time and replacing them with high quality fakes, but she'd had enough of this life. She wanted to be rich again, as she had once been. And *you can bet your ass that I won't be losing it to another pretty boy this time.*

"So what do you say, Natalia? Are you interested?" asked Gerald once he had outlined the plan. "Alex has authorized me to offer you one hundred thousand dollars a year."

"One hundred thousand dollars a year?" asked the old movie star. It was a fortune, and she knew it, but it wasn't nearly close to what she had in mind. She picked up a strawberry from the bowl on the occasional table and studied it. "I'm sorry," she said, "that's not nearly enough." And then she popped the berry in her mouth.

If it had been anybody else, they would surely have been stunned, but Gerald was not surprised in the least. This was Natalia, and he knew her well enough to know she had something in mind. "So what is it that you want, Natalia?"

"I want to become a partner," she said, and after a long struggle and some hard negotiations, she got her deal.

"Welcome on board," said Alex to his new vice-president of public relations, sounding none too pleased. "You'd better be worth the money we'll be paying you."

"Don't worry dahhhrling," she replied. "I'll be worth my weight in gold." And of all the board members, she laughed the loudest and the longest.

Natalia rose to the challenge with fervor. She got on the telephone and within days she was booked on every popular television talk show in the city. Once she had made the rounds of New York, she headed west to Los Angeles and made the round out there.

She sat before the camera in a tight size 22 dress with a deep *décolleté*, and flashed her world-famous thirty carat Canary diamond, the only real stone she had not sold. "It would be a crime to tear down the Grand Palace," she told Dina Merill who nodded her approval. "Why I remember when I was just starting at MGM, Joan Crawford had her spring ball there one year. Everyone came. Howard Hughes was there. I remember..." She went on with story after story of the glamorous events that took place there.

She appealed to the public and they responded in droves. Letters arrived by the bags full at Power Properties, some of them with donations, which were immediately sent back, along with a thank you note and a signed autograph of Natalia. One month later, Alex went back to see the mayor.

"You again." The man said when he recognized Alex. "I thought I told you..."

Alex interrupted him. "I believe you might be interested in seeing this." He signaled to the delivery boy who followed a few steps behind him. The boy left and reappeared moments later with two mail bags full of letters which he promptly emptied on the mayor's desk. Envelopes flooded the top of the desk and spilled over onto the floor.

Alex smiled innocently. "I have seven more of these bags out in the hall. Would you like me to have them brought in?"

"No! No!" The major was trying to push the mass of envelopes back into the empty bags. "This is ridiculous. Get those out of here. I have a meeting with the election committee in a few minutes."

"I think you have some serious thinking to do," continued Alex with a grin. "I would estimate that you have at least two thousand letters here. That represents two thousand of your constituents. Another fourteen thousand are in the bags out in the hall. Those are all people who won't vote for you at the next election if you insist on tearing down that hotel." Alex pulled out his card and handed it to the mayor. "I would really like to help you get re-elected. Think about it." He walked out.

The next morning, Alex was at his desk when his secretary buzzed him. "There's a call for you from the mayor on line one."

Alex picked up the phone. "Hello Mr. Mayor. What can I do for you today?"

The answer came back clearly over the static of the line. "I've given some thought to your idea. I think maybe we should talk."

One month later the *New York Times* carried the story on the front page of the Saturday edition.

NEW YORK LANDMARK
SAVED FROM DESTRUCTION.

MAYOR WANTS GRAND
PALACE TO BE RESTORED.

Underneath in smaller captions, followed the story of the famous hotel and of the company that had bought it with the intention of restoring it to its previous glamour.

* * * * *

Chapter 8

Anne Turner was having breakfast in the kitchen of her new home. Across from her sat her husband, deeply focused on the newspaper he was reading. She took another sip of her coffee and sighed. "Why did you marry me if you can't even bother to say two words to me in the morning?"

Her new husband pushed his bifocals back up his nose and kept reading.

She leaned back and folded her arms across her chest. "Harry! I'm talking to you. Harry, look at me when I'm talking to you. I'm your wife, for Chrissake!"

Harry put down his newspaper wearily.

"Believe me, dear; that is something I wish I could forget."

Anne's face turned a deep shade of red and she sat up straight. "And what is that supposed to mean?"

"It simply means dear, that you remind me of that fact constantly."

"Oh." She let herself fall back against her chair. "Well, I expect you to behave like a husband. I don't want to have to look at a newspaper every morning at breakfast. If I'd wanted that, I would simply have bought my own subscription to the *New York Times*. I would like to see your face once in a while."

"Anne, I don't know what you want from me. You asked me to marry you. I did! You said you wanted me to legally adopt your son. I did! You asked for a new house. I bought it! You said you needed a fur coat. You got it! Now I ask you. Would you kindly just let me read my paper in peace?" He picked up his newspaper again and resumed his reading.

Anne glared at the newspaper. She was just about to add a few sharp words when a picture on the front page caught her eye. She leaned forward and looked at it more closely. "Let me see that." She grabbed the front section from Harry and began to read. The expression of disbelief on her face slowly transformed into one of pure fury. "That fucking son of a bitch. I don't believe this!"

"What? Who are you talking about?"

"Him!" Anne shrieked back. "That son of a bitch, Alex Ivanov. He..." She started to explain then stopped herself in time.

"You know him?"

"Know him? I guess you could say that. He owes me some money," she said. She looked up at her husband and stopped. "Oh, it wasn't that much, and it was a long time ago." And she quickly changed the subject.

* * * * *

CHAPTER 9

The announcement that Power Properties, headed by Alex Ivanov, was to restore the Grand Palace to its original splendor, set off a flurry of publicity. Suddenly, it seemed that the main question around town was, 'Who *is* Alex Ivanov?' *Time* magazine did a two-page story about 'The Man With the Power: His New Hotel and Casino,' and almost overnight Alex's name became famous.

Everywhere he went, people recognized him from his picture in the paper. "That's Alex Ivanov," they whispered to one another as they vied for a closer look. Alex went about his business, pretending not to notice. To those close to him, he complained about the lack of privacy.

"It's like living in a damn fish bowl. Who needs it?" In reality, he loved every minute of it. And when the awestruck stranger who noticed him, also happened to be a beautiful young woman, he loved it even more.

Reporters and readers alike were fascinated. Alex Ivanov was a true American hero, a man who had come from nowhere and had climbed the ladder to immense success and wealth. Alex, eager to believe his own publicity, devoured every article. When one magazine described his style of dressing as conservative and uninspired, Alex was so upset, he couldn't sleep that night. As huge as his ego had become, it was equally fragile. The day after the article with the negative comment, he went out and bought an entirely new wardrobe.

"What you need are clothes that spell power, if you'll pardon the pun," said the salesclerk, a stunning brunette with smoldering eyes. "You want your suits to be dark and expensive-looking. Your shirts should be crisp and well made. And your ties, they must be bold and dramatic. After all, a man's tie is his phallic symbol. You wouldn't want a wishy-washy looking tie, now would you?"

When Alex stepped out of the changing room, the pretty clerk nodded emphatically. "Now!" she said. "Now you look like the rich and powerful man that you are. By the way," she added. "Here's my telephone number. You never know when you might need some help... with your wardrobe?" The message was unmistakable.

Since Alex had ended the affair with Susan Temple years ago, his marriage had improved for a time, but instead of making him feel better, being in a close and loving relationship had only made him feel more uncomfortable. He was a married man, but instead of fairytale wedded bliss, he felt more like a man imprisoned. The more his wife tried to please him, the more he felt as though she was his jailer. His solution had been to have a continuous string of one-night stands. In this way, he was able to prove to himself that he was still free. Nobody could dictate to Alex Ivanov what he could do and what he couldn't. Not even his own wedding vows.

Alex looked at the pretty clerk and felt the familiar rush of sexual excitement. He took the piece of paper and tucked it safely away in his billfold. "By any chance, would you happen to be free for dinner tonight?" he asked.

The next morning Brigitte sat on the bed and watched as her husband took inordinate care in the knotting of his new, bright red tie. "Hmmm!

You look good. Don't let any pretty young thing get her claws into you," she said with a twinkle in her eyes.

"Oh for Chrissake, Brigitte! My image is important. If I want people to know I'm successful, I have to look successful."

His angry reaction surprised her. "Is it so important that people know you have money?" she asked.

"Money is power, my dear, and don't you ever believe otherwise," he answered, exasperated. *And power is the best aphrodisiac in the world*, he thought, remembering the sales clerk and her insatiable appetite the night before. *What a lay she was!* His prick grew to half-mast as he thought of the adoring look in her eyes. Although he had been tempted, he had wisely decided not to see her again. After Susan Temple, he had vowed to never get involved with another woman. But a fling, that was not getting involved, and Brigitte would never find out about it.

He finished the last loop of his tie and stepped back to study the results. Satisfied, he turned back to Brigitte. "You know, you should pay more attention to what you wear too. After all, the way my wife looks is a direct reflection on me."

After he left, Brigitte studied herself in the mirror. *When was the last time Alex told me I look beautiful?* she wondered, and could not remember. *I'm still attractive.* Her face was still beautiful, her skin soft and smooth. Her figure was slender, her breasts firm and full.

Incredibly, seven years had gone by since she and Alex had married. Five years since that terrible day she had found out about his affair, and had resigned herself to end her own career. Although she still missed her art, she felt strongly that devoting herself to her husband had been the right thing to do. *My marriage is solid. If there is one thing I can be sure of, it's Alex's loyalty.* A sudden sadness washed over her. *If only I could have given Alex children of his own.* But there had been no other children after David. The dozens of fertility specialists she had visited in her quest to give Alex a child, had made it clear that she could never become pregnant again. Unfortunately, she only had herself to blame. The infection she had suffered from her attempted abortion so many years ago, had left her barren. Memories came flashing back. She was in a bath full of hot water, pushing a wire deep inside herself. The sudden gush of blood. Then Marcel and the hospital. *God forgive me for that.* She pushed the nightmarish memory away and picked up the telephone.

"Natalia? I need your help. I think it's time I started looking more... you know... elegant." She listened for a moment. "No of course Alex is not criticizing me again. This is my own idea. Now, tell me, where should I start?"

With Natalia's help she went shopping, and within a few months, photographs of the new, more fashionable Brigitte Ivanov began appearing in all the leading magazines. She was shown in *Ladies' Home Journal*, inspecting the kitchen of the Grand Palace, dressed in a white Courrège outfit complete with white kid gloves and shoes. For *Good Housekeeping,* she wore a green silk evening dress and posed behind a lavishly decorated Thanksgiving dinner table. For *Vogue*, she went all out and took the crew on a tour of the new home she and Alex had bought, and for every shot, she wore a different designer gown.

Their new house was a sprawling white stone mansion, set on five acres of impeccably groomed land. Black shutters framed every window, and double pillars graced the sides of the massive carved front door above which Alex had hung a large, golden eagle. Inside, there were twelve bedrooms, including a master suite, complete with his and hers bathrooms and dressing rooms. The dining room comfortably sat forty, and the living room was the size of a hotel salon.

"From now on Réjeanne, I want you to feel like the mistress of the house," Brigitte had told her when they moved in. "And I don't want to see you lift a finger." Réjeanne was given a private suite of her own, with large bath and living area, and she was replaced by a staff of five. There was an upstairs maid, a downstairs maid, a cook, a butler and a driver for the new stretch limousine.

"I don't know, Brigitte," Réjeanne replied hesitantly. "I'm not used to all this. I don't like having a stranger in my kitchen, and every time I turn around, someone is dusting and vacuuming my room. What am I supposed to do with myself?"

"Enjoy life," said Brigitte firmly. "You are as much my family as Alex and David are. I don't want to see you working anymore."

But Réjeanne simply took over the role of housekeeper and harassed the staff continuously. If so much as a speck of dust was discovered, the servant responsible for that area was immediately dispatched to 'get rid of that dirt'. Under Réjeanne's sharp eye, the house was kept immaculate.

"I want this house to be a showplace," Alex had told Brigitte after the signing. "God knows I have more than enough money to spend on decorating it. Why don't you try to fix it up?"

How interesting that he calls it a house rather than home. Nevertheless Brigitte threw herself into the project with abandon. She hunted down the top antique and art dealers, and filled the house with priceless pieces.

When she suggested putting up a few of her own paintings, Alex vehemently refused. "Don't be ridiculous. I want important pieces! Collector pieces. None of that modern crap!" His words stung, but Brigitte set to work. Soon, there were Degas, Matisses and Monets everywhere. In the dining room, the chandelier was of Czarist Russia. The pieces of furniture were original antiques from France, Austria and Germany. The rugs were heirlooms, and on the wall were priceless tapestries and hand-painted silks.

"This is the single most expensive private home in the area," Alex boasted to anyone who would listen. "I spent millions to decorate it. Everything is the best that money can buy."

Brigitte cringed every time. *I wish he would care as much about us, as he does about his image*, she thought sadly.

But that was Alex, and she had vowed to love him as he was.

• • • • •

CHAPTER 10

The publicity machine droned on. One could scarcely walk by a newsstand without being confronted by at least a half dozen covers featuring both or either half of America's fairy-tale couple. Alexander and Brigitte Ivanov had become the American equivalent of royalty.

They were in the sitting area off the master bedroom. Alex was reading one of the many magazines featuring an article about Brigitte that month. "What the hell is the matter with those reporters? They paid more attention to your clothes than to our four million dollar house."

Brigitte put down her book. "You asked me to

be more visible. Isn't that what you wanted?" she asked, surprised.

"They never even mentioned me in the article," Alex grumbled sullenly. He flung the magazine across the room and stormed out.

Brigitte was stunned. *What does he want from me?* She picked up the pile of magazines on the coffee table and flipped through them quickly. She was 'The woman behind the man,' in one magazine; 'The most stylish woman in America in another, and New York's most gracious hostess' in yet another. She had stood by her husband during interviews, smiled and talked about their perfect marriage. She had done everything Alex asked of her. Instead of being a person in her own right, she lived in the shadow of her husband—the dutiful wife, no more than an accessory on his arm.

Her only refusal had been when Alex suggested allowing David to be photographed. Brigitte had put her foot down

"No! Absolutely not! I will not let my son be used for publicity reasons." Alex had been furious, but in the end he had no choice but to accept his wife's decision. David was, after all, Brigitte's son.

Brigitte put away the magazines and wandered

downstairs to the sun room where David was adding the finishing touches to his latest painting. David Alexander Dartois was fourteen years old, tall and slender like his mother. And like Brigitte, he also had the ability to put paint onto a canvas and make a picture come to life.

"That is good!" exclaimed Brigitte from the doorway. The painting was of a sunset over a wide expanse of wheat fields. Even from a distance she could see that the oil had strength, yet suggested a peaceful feeling. She walked over for a closer look. "It's really very good! How would you like me to hang it in the library?"

"Would you?" asked the boy, thrilled with the idea. "But how would Alex feel about that?" he added uncertainly.

"I can't imagine why he would object."

A few days later, when the oil had dried, Brigitte took the painting out to be framed, and one week later it was hanging above the fireplace in the library. That night at dinner, Brigitte could hardly wait for Alex to finish his meal. "David has a surprise for you in the library," she said. "Follow me."

"I don't have time right now," Alex answered sullenly as he wiped his mouth with his napkin. "I have a meeting and unless I leave now, I'll be late."

Brigitte saw the disappointment on her son's face. "Oh please, Alex. It will only take a minute," she insisted, sending her husband a pleading look.

"Only for a minute," he relented. Alex followed Brigitte and David grudgingly into the room.

"What's that?" asked Alex when he noticed the painting.

David stood by nervously while Alex inspected it.

"So what do you think?" asked Brigitte eagerly.

"It's not bad," answered Alex. "But I don't know what the big deal is. We have Renoirs and Matisses all over the house. We even have a Rembrandt in the dining room. I've never even heard of..." He leaned forward to read the signature. "Who the hell is D.E.D.?"

"David Etienne Dartois," said David softly. He watched the surprise on Alex's face. "Do you like it?" he asked, full of hope.

"Yes," said Alex, still stunned. "I do. It's very good David." He gave the boy an affectionate slap on the back. "Now you go on off to do your homework. Your mother and I have a few things we need to talk about."

"O.K." answered David easily. "But you really mean it? You like my painting?"

"Yes I do, David. It's very nice. Now you be a good boy, and leave us alone for a minute."

David felt so happy, he thought he might explode. *He likes my painting.* It was the first time Alex had ever paid him a compliment. "Sure. Night *Maman*. Night Alex." He trudged out of the room beaming from his stepfather's compliment.

As soon as David was out of earshot, Alex turned back to Brigitte. "Why are you encouraging him this way?" he demanded angrily.

Brigitte was aghast. "But Alex, what harm is there in encouraging David in an area in which he is so obviously talented?"

"David has enormous potential. He's brilliant. He doesn't even try and he gets straight A's in all his classes at college. He could do so much with his life. Why the hell would you want him to be a stupid artist? I think it's time I started taking an interest in your son's activities. Just because you wanted to be an artist, is no reason for you to try and steer David in that direction. And frankly, his painting is not bad, but I certainly don't think it's brilliant."

Before Brigitte could say a word, Alex had left.

A moment later she heard the front door close. Exhaustion washed over her, leaving her feeling helpless. No matter how hard she tried, nothing she did ever pleased her husband. She slumped into a chair, and began to cry.

"Don't cry *Maman*."

She looked up, startled. "David! What are you doing here?"

"I-I was outside..."

"Oh David." Brigitte was heartbroken. "Don't tell me you overheard."

David smiled weakly. "It's O.K. I don't mind. I know Alex loves me and he only wants what's best for me."

Brigitte opened her arms. "Come here *mon chéri*." She wrapped her arms around him. "You're right. Alex does love you. But you don't have to be anything you don't want to be. You are absolutely perfect just the way you are." For a long time, Brigitte sat there, cradling her nearly grown-up son. It felt so incredibly wonderful, holding him and hugging him like that. It had been way too long since the last time she had done that. "Have I told you lately how much I love you?" she asked.

David chuckled. "Oh Mom! You tell me all the time."

* * * * *

The official reopening of the Grand Palace was scheduled for the first of June. The event was planned with the meticulous detailing of a royal coronation. On the evening of the opening ball, guests were greeted at the door by a dozen well-built young men, dressed in official looking bright red British guard uniforms, complete with swords and tall fur hats. Inside, a stiff and formal-looking butler carefully inspected each invitation before guiding the guests toward a majordomo who called out the names of every new arrival to the packed ballroom below. "Mr. and Mrs. Hemsley," he called out, his voice booming above the gentle strains of the string quartet in the far corner of the room. "Mr. and Mrs. Forbes."

Alex beamed, resplendent in his tuxedo. Brigitte wore a soft blue taffeta and tulle creation sprinkled with rhinestones, and looked every bit the fairy-tale princess the press continuously likened her to. She smiled and shook hands with each guest, struggling to keep faces and names together. "Good evening Mr. Forbes. It was good of you to come. Mrs. Forbes, what a beautiful gown. Is it a Dior?"

With a toss of her head and a tight little smile the woman replied. "Yes, of course. I won't wear anything but French designs..."

Mr. Forbes turned his attention to Alex. "Call me Malcolm, please. Great job, you've done here."

"Thank you Malcolm."

"The way you're going, young man, you'll be making my Fortune Five Hundred list someday soon."

"I sure plan to, Malcolm. I sure do plan to."

Gerald Masson and his new girlfriend—a tall, thin brunette by the name of Carla—Andrew McGregor and Natalia Berenson completed the receiving line. Natalia, all two hundred and fifty pounds of her, looked stunning in her usual double thickness of false lashes and a black sequined Bob Mackie gown.

"You look absolutely gorgeous," said Brigitte to Natalia as soon as the last guest had gone by to join the crowd below. She couldn't help stealing curious glances at Carla.

"It just goes to show! You can never have too

much of a good thing," Natalia replied with a deep throaty laugh, sending her body jiggling.

"You're absolutely right," added Alex, thinking of the profits he would make on the Royal Palace. "You can never have too much of a good thing." He noticed the reporter for the *New York Times* and rushed off to join him. "Did you visit the royal suite?" he asked him. "Did you get the photographer to take pictures of the lobby?" he continued. "What a monument to myself! I ask you. What can I ever do to beat this?"

"I don't know," replied the reporter as he scribbled down Alex's comments. "But I'm sure you'll think of something Mr. Ivanov."

After dinner, the string quartet was replaced by a rock and roll band. For the rest of the evening, the women hitched up their long skirts and the men shed their dinner jackets, and they all danced the night away to the modern sounds of The Beatles 'Hard Day's Night', the Rolling Stones 'No Satisfaction', and The Beach Boys 'Surf City'. Never had such a glittering crowd had such fun.

Brigitte watched indulgently as Alex boogied, gyrated and grooved with one attractive guest after another. After an energetic rock and roll number, he hurried back to the table. "Gerald, you don't mind if I steal this lovely lady from you"

"Be my guest," replied Gerald, and he watched them make their way to the dance floor. He had seen the way Carla had been flirting with Alex during the evening; and he also knew Alex well enough to realize that he would not resist. *I guess I might as well forget her number.*

Over the years, Gerald had become aware of Alex's numerous infidelities and had often struggled with his desire to tell Brigitte. In the end, he had decided that would be a mistake. Alex's behavior was so flagrant that if Brigitte did not know by now, it could only be because she did not want to know. *If she were my wife*, he thought. *I wouldn't want any other woman.* He had long ago abandoned any idea of a relationship with Brigitte. She was married and very loyal to her husband. But even more important, he would not have been comfortable having an affair with a married woman. *Of course if ever Alex and Brigitte were to divorce, that would be a different story.* He looked at Brigitte again and leaned in toward her. "Would you care to join me on the dance floor?" he asked. The band had just picked up the first few chords of Roll Over Beethoven.

"Thanks Gerald. I think I'd rather just sit this one out if you don't mind."

"Did you know that one of this hotel's greatest patrons used to be Marjorie Meriwether Post?" he continued, in an effort to draw Brigitte into a conversation.

"I had no idea," she answered politely.

"She must be rolling over in her grave tonight," he said, and suddenly felt overwhelmed with love for the wife of his partner. For years now, he had kept a safe distance from Brigitte, out of respect for both her and her husband. He had even tried to develop relationships with other women, but invariably, thoughts of his partner's wife interfered. *Brigitte must be aware of the way I feel about her.* "Have I told you how beautiful you look tonight?" he asked.

"Thank you Gerald." Brigitte hesitated for a moment. Then she put her hand on his arm and continued. "You are a dear friend. I hope we shall always be dear friends." The words were affectionate, but the meaning behind them was clear. She wanted nothing more than friendship from her husband's partner. Gerald sighed and turned his attention back to the crowd of dancers as they boogied to the music. Brigitte sat quietly. *If only Alex were more like Gerald*, she though, feeling guilty for feeling disappointed in her marriage. Lately it seemed to weigh heavily on her mind.

The ball ended as the first rays of morning sun rose above the city. After a champagne, scrambled eggs and caviar breakfast, the guests began to leave the hotel in a procession of Rolls Royces and limousines.

After everyone had departed, Alex joined Brigitte, Gerald and Carla at the table. "What a great party!" he exclaimed. "New York hasn't seen a party like this in years."

"So Alex, now that the Grand Palace is completed, what will Power Properties do for an encore?" asked Carla, her eyes full of admiration.

"I'll find something," answered Alex, importantly. "Believe me, I'll find something."

Alex did not search for long. At the next board meeting, he made the announcement to his vice-presidents. "In answer to the question everyone is asking," he said, beaming with excitement. "Power Properties' next project is to build the largest and most luxurious casino in America. How is that for an encore?"

"A casino? Are you crazy? Why would we want to get involved with gambling?" asked Gerald, stunned.

"Why? Because, casinos are the best way to make a legal killing. One casino will make more money in one year than the Grand Palace can make in a hundred years."

Andrew McGregor looked at Gerald. "You know Alex," he said, shrugging. "Once he has his mind set on something..."

"I know, I know," replied Gerald. "And what will we call this casino?"

Alex grinned. "The Power Hotel and Casino, what else?"

It took nearly a year of legal wrangling until the permit for the casino was issued, and another two years for the construction to be completed. When it opened, The Power, as the newspapers referred to it, was the single most luxurious hotel casino in the country. The lobby alone had cost over two million dollars with pink Italian marble specially flown in from Italy and gold-plated fixtures from Germany. There were three restaurants, one to cater to every taste and budget. "And the best one," had said Alex to his wife when he showed her the plans. "Will be a French restaurant called 'Brigitte's.' How do you like that sweetheart?"

"I love it!" exclaimed Brigitte. "And I love you,

mon chéri." This time, for a change, he returned her admiring look. Sometimes Alex would surprise her and do something entirely unexpected and totally romantic.

At the Power Hotel and Casino, every one of the one thousand bedrooms on the thirty floors above was exquisitely decorated. Alex had convinced Brigitte to supervise the decorating of the hotel, and she had done him proud. The furniture was elegant and tasteful. The bedspreads and window dressings were of the finest materials. The pillows were goose-down. The towels were thick Egyptian cotton. Even the sheets were nothing less than Pratesi. "I want nothing but the best for my casino," said Alex repeatedly to his reluctant board of directors as he approved every luxurious detail. "I want it to be known that Alex Ivanov will spare no expense to make his guests feel comfortable." Six months after the official opening, The Power Hotel and Casino was the largest-grossing casino in Atlantic City. "What did I tell you?" he asked Andrew McGregor, who had loudly objected to the enormous expenditures. "You have to spend money, to make money."

· · · · ·

CHAPTER 11

The offices of Power Properties had changed considerably over the years. There was now a large reception area with pearl grey wall-to-wall carpeting and ultra-suede upholstered furniture. There was a projection room where potential buyers were shown a ten minute promotional film about the many projects of the company with the velvety voice of Frank Sinatra's *'New York, New York'* in the background. There were elegant but efficient secretaries and assistants, answering telephones and running around taking dictation and typing letters. Some days, Alex would walk in and stop, amazed. *I did it*, he would tell himself. *Everything I wanted to achieve, I achieved. What more can I possibly want?* The answer was invariably the same. *More! I want more!*

• • • • •

They were sitting around the boardroom table, discussing possible new projects.

"Why don't we build hotels," asked Natalia. "With the experience we've earned with The Power Hotel and Casino, building more hotels would be the natural next step."

"I've heard the Excellence chain of hotels is having some financial problems. Maybe we should look into it," added Andrew.

"What do you say, Alex?" asked Gerald Masson. "I'm almost sorry I sold my own hotels twelve years ago. If I'd known Power Properties might someday be interested in hotels, I would have held on to them and made myself a billion dollars selling them to Alex."

"I have an idea," said Alex, not amused. He paused for a moment, enjoying the way his vice-presidents grew silent as they respectfully waited for his opinion. "I think it's time New York got the tallest, most beautiful and most expensive luxury apartment building the world has ever seen."

Natalia shook her head. "Be reasonable Alex. New York has plenty of luxury buildings."

"Nothing like what I have in mind."

The following month, Alex announced to the

world his plans to build Power Building. It would be one hundred stories high . The exterior would be entirely covered with smoky glass. Inside, there would be an atrium, complete with waterfalls, a jungle of tropical plants, rolling brass escalators, and a few dozen small, but very exclusive boutiques that would cater to the most discerning of shoppers. The apartments would be the most expensive the world had ever seen; private elevators for the tenants, indoor swimming pools, living rooms with sunken floors. There would be private exercise rooms, ballrooms, even a landing pad on the roof for helicopters.

One year before it was completed, the Power Building was sold out. Word had leaked out that Khashoggi had bought an entire floor, and that Gloria Vanderbilt had reserved the penthouse. Almost overnight, the Power Building had become the trendy address for the rich and famous.

• • • • •

Fame and fortune, Alex believed, were the keys that opened all doors. Since his early success with The Grand Palace, invitations from clubs and organizations and social cliques kept pouring in.

They were sorting through the usual number of invitations in the room Alex called 'the library.' In reality, it was no more than a large, mahogany-paneled room with wall-to-wall bookcases filled with priceless sculptures, a variety of heavy silver-framed photographs of Alex with other famous people, and a few books.

"I have single handedly doubled the value of New York real estate," Alex boasted proudly. "How's that for an encore? Now, you tell me. What can I do to beat that?"

"You'll think of something," answered Brigitte. *Unfortunately, you'll surely think of something.* Over the years, Alex had changed. It had been impossible not to notice and nearly impossible to ignore. But Brigitte had grown used to keeping her thoughts to herself.

Instead of making him happy and content, his achievements seemed to leave him dissatisfied. He was a man possessed, always wanting more, and more, and more. *When will this madness end?*

"A few years ago, these people would not have given us the time of day," said Alex, shaking his head in amazement at the dozens of invitations before him.

"I know," answered Brigitte. "It makes me wonder how honest some of those friendships really are."

"Don't be so *naïve*. All it means is that I have worked damned hard, and that people are giving me the respect I deserve." He paused for a moment then continued. "You know, I think we should think about getting a swimming pool. If we want to entertain properly in the summer, we'll need one."

"I-I don't know Alex. With David's heart condition, wouldn't that just be encouraging him to participate in an activity he really shouldn't be doing?"

"For Chrissake, Brigitte," Alex exploded. "I am so fed up with hearing about David's heart condition. The boy is perfectly healthy and he is nearly seventeen years old. When are you going to let him have a normal life?"

"I-I am ..."

"You call it normal that a boy his age is not allowed to do sports? You call it normal that you still drive him to school every day and won't ever allow him to go on vacation with his friends. He should be playing tennis, going out with girls. Instead, you keep him cooped up inside, painting. You are the worst kind of a mother. You are so damned selfish, you convince yourself your son wants a career as an artist simply because that's what you wanted for yourself. You are living your life vicariously through David."

Alex's harsh words stung and Brigitte struggled to keep from crying. "That is an outright lie. David is a very gifted artist. I only want to encourage his talent. If he wanted to do something else with his life, I would certainly not stand in his way."

"As far as I'm concerned, David is probably the closest I will ever come to having a son. Have you ever given any thought to what I might want for him? I run a multi-million dollar empire. Maybe I'd like to groom him to take over someday."

Brigitte's head was spinning. Alex had never mentioned any interest in preparing David for such an eventuality. If anything, Alex had seemed to lose interest in David over the years. Lately, the two were no more than polite strangers.

Alex was still livid. "I want a swimming pool, and I'm going to get one. And furthermore, David is going to learn to swim."

A few days later when the designers arrived, Alex greeted them at the door with dozens of pictures and drawings of lavish swimming pools.

"I want a big one, and I want it to look expensive," he told the men.

Two months later, the work on the swimming pool was completed. "It's Olympic size," explained the proud contractor as he handed Alex the bill. "Fully heated so the temperature will never dip beneath a comfortable 85°."

"And more important," added Alex, laughing proudly. "It's the most damned expensive swimming pool around."

* * * * *

David had grown into a fine young man. For years his epilepsy had been kept under tight control. There were dozens of pills and countless visits to the doctor and always, the explanation to everyone about David's 'heart condition'.

Over the years, Brigitte had developed a knack for being able to predict whenever David was about to have a seizure. Before an episode, he was just a bit quieter, a little less outgoing and less able to concentrate. Whenever Brigitte noticed those signs in David, it was her signal to keep him away from classes that day. Luckily, the few episodes that did occur, happened at home where Brigitte and Réjeanne were able to care for him, away from the rabid eyes of the press. His condition was monitored regularly and his dosage of medicine increased whenever it was deemed necessary. David's epilepsy was kept so secret that even Alex was unaware of it.

One week after construction on the pool was completed, Alex hired a swimming instructor and called David to the library. "Here's the schedule," he said as he handed him a typewritten sheet. "From now on, you'll be taking lessons every day after classes. We'll have you ready for the Olympics before you know it."

David waited until Alex left. "Mom," he said as soon as he was alone with her. "I don't want to take swimming lessons. I'd rather use that time for painting. There's this new technique I'm practicing..."

"I understand sweetheart, but you know Alex. When he sets his mind to something, nothing can change it. Why don't you just give it a try for a little while? Don't worry; you'll still have plenty of time for your painting."

But Alex had other plans for what remained of David's free time. Over dinner a few nights later,

Alex made his announcement. "Son," he said as he pushed away his untouched plate. "I've been thinking about what you should do with your summer vacations this year. I've decided you'll be spending them with me."

David looked at Alex, stunned. His stepfather had never addressed him in that way before. "Wh-what do you mean?"

Alex wiped his mouth on the lace linen napkin and explained. "I think it's high time you started doing something constructive with your life. From now on, you're going to learn about the business world. I am officially hiring you as my junior assistant at Power Properties. Can you think of a better learning experience than that?"

* * * * *

Chapter 12

Anne Turner sat before her husband's lawyer, in shock.

The lawyer, a wrinkled old man with a hair piece, was saying, "From what I can see, your husband spent every last penny he had. At the rate he was spending, another few months and he would have been bankrupt. As horrible as this may sounds, one could say he was lucky he died when he did."

"This-this can't be," she exclaimed, horrified. "What did he do with all his money? He had millions."

The old lawyer hesitated. "My dear lady," he said gently to the stricken widow. "Your husband loved you very much, and he demonstrated his love very generously over the years." He shook his full head of fake hair sadly and continued. "Unfortunately, Harry never took my advice. I don't know how many times I told him to be more careful with his spending. But Harry never wanted you to know that his fortune was dwindling."

For an instant, Anne thought of the vast amounts of money Harry had spent on her over the years—all those exotic trips, the numerous pieces of expensive jewelry and the endless shopping sprees at the designer salons. *Why didn't I get him to buy real estate, she asked herself bitterly. At least that would be worth something now.*

After the meeting, Anne Turner jumped into her Porsche Carrera and drove back home with engine roaring and tires screeching. Inside, the house was dark and quiet. Anne ran from room to room, flipping on lights and turning on radios and televisions. In the living room she stopped before the picture of her deceased husband. Suddenly she started trembling. First her hands, then the shaking spread to her knees, to her legs, until it had taken over her entire body. Eighteen years, she had spent with him. *Eighteen. long, fucking years, waiting for the bastard to die. And now this!* "Why the hell did you fall behind in your life-insurance payments?" she screamed, her voice echoing through the empty rooms. "You told me you were rich! If I had known this, I would never have married you."

She turned away abruptly and ran to the bedroom. She fell to her knees in front of her open closet and began to pull out shoes and boots, throwing them angrily across the room. *There it is!* She picked up the shoe box and carried it back to the living room.

One by one, she pulled them out. There were hundreds of them, articles and pictures of Alexander Ivanov, his wife Brigitte, and the boy David. Anne stared at the boy for a long time. Then she began to scream. "He's not even your flesh and blood, you damn bastard. You should have married me!" She grew silent again as her mind tried to think.

The front door opened and closed, but Anne did not hear it. She picked up the issue of *Fortune* magazine with Alex on the cover. "I hate you!" she screamed. Her hands began tearing the magazine into shreds. I hate you! I hate you! I hate you!" she kept screaming as she tore through the stack of articles and papers, scattering them across the room.

The Sting of the Scorpio

A shadow fell on her and she turned around, her makeup streaked from the angry tears.

"Mom! Are you all right?"

"What are you doing here?" she demanded hoarsely. "You're supposed to be at college."

"I just heard about Harry. Why didn't you call me? I should have been here, with you."

Anne turned away and looked at the remains of her collection.

"What are those?" asked the boy, as he noticed the mess.

Anne Turner looked at her son, her eyes full of venom. "Do you recognize him?" she asked.

"Yes sure. Who wouldn't?" he answered puzzled.

"He's your father."

"Wh-what?"

"You heard me. He's your father. And he is stealing your birthright away from you."

For a long time that night, Richard thought about the story his mother had told him. If what she said was true, he was the illegitimate son, but the only flesh and blood son, of one of the richest men in America. *Wow!* he thought. *There's got to be some way I can get my hands on some of that dough.*

• • • • •

CHAPTER 13

Although it had been founded on real estate, Power Properties had diversified and expanded all over the United States until it now owned two casinos, a chain of luxury hotels, a variety of co-op and condominium projects and of course, the jewel of the Power Properties collection, the Power Properties Tower.

They were sitting in the boardroom. Alex was saying, "The Royal Victoria is a floating palace. It's the largest ship in the Cameron fleet. Lucky for us, Bernie Cameron is having a few problems lately." He laughed. "Let's just say that the old fox was outfoxed," he said, referring to the man's sharp young wife who had filed for divorce and sued for half of Bernie Cameron's fortune.

David looked across the table to Gerald, Andrew and Natalia. Nobody was saying a word.

"So what do you think David?" asked Alex.

David nodded. "Sounds good." *Some people's misfortune...* he thought morosely. It had been six years since Alex had made his announcement over dinner that night—six long years, since he had grudgingly joined Power Properties and ended all hopes of ever becoming a serious artist. It was true, as Alex continuously reminded him, that he would most probably have made very little money as an artist. Instead, he now he had his private office at Power Properties and an impressive gold plate on the door that said, **David E. Dartois, vice-president**. In reality he was no more than a glamorized gofer. He followed Alex around from meeting to meeting, listened to endless discussions and multi-million dollar negotiations, and in return for his occasional opinion, which was never adopted, he took home a six figure salary, an impressive figure for a twenty-three year old. He would still have preferred being a struggling artist.

Alex kept talking. "So Bernie's got a bit of a cash flow problem right now. It's an incredible opportunity for Power Properties. So here's the deal," he said and pulled out a thick folder from his alligator briefcase. "The Royal Victoria is conservatively valued at six hundred million dollars and Bernie had to mortgage two hundred million of it to try and save his fleet. He hasn't made a payment in seven months, and they are sweating bullets over at the bank. I spoke to the president of the bank and they have already begun foreclosing procedures, and," he added after a dramatic pause. "They are willing to sell to us for the balance of the mortgage."

Gerald Masson raised his eyebrows. "You mean the whole deal will cost us only two hundred mill?"

"Right!"

Andrew let out a long low whistle. "I can't see how we can possibly turn it down. The only problem is that we're not very liquid at the moment. Just how do you propose to make the payments?"

"The bank is willing to give us six months before the first payment. That gives us plenty of time to get the advertising department to do their stuff. I want the Royal Victoria to be known as the world's most luxurious floating casino."

Natalia's heavily made-up eyes nearly popped out of her head. "You're transforming the Royal Victoria into a casino?"

Alex's chest puffed out proudly. "You bet. Can you think of any way to make the Royal Victoria more profitable than that?"

"My God, it's almost sacrilegious," said Natalia. "But I have to admit, it's brilliant. We'll be in international waters, so we don't have to worry about gambling licenses."

Andrew nodded. "Getting regulated won't be nearly as complicated as it was for Atlantic City."

"Do I assume everyone's in favor?" asked Alex, his eyes going over the group.

"In favor," said Andrew.

"In favor," said David and Gerald simultaneously.

"I better get to the advertising department and start working on this," said Natalia as she heaved herself out of her chair. "Alex, I've got to hand it to you, you're brilliant. I'll try and get you a few ideas by tomorrow afternoon."

The meeting came to a close and the rest of the group rose from the table.

Just as David was leaving the room, Alex called out to him. "Oh David, I have another meeting I have to go to. Can you tell your mother I'll be home late?"

"Sure Alex," answered David, his face carefully blank. For years, there had been an endless series of late night 'meetings'. "I'll tell her."

* * * * *

A few hours later, the long black limousine wove its way through the traffic. In the back, Alex was pouring two glasses of champagne. He handed one to the pretty blonde in the tight red jumpsuit. "To you," he said. "And the best blow job I ever got in my entire life." He lifted his glass and drank.

"To more good times," said the girl, and she took a sip. She put down her glass on the mahogany sideboard and smiled seductively. "So when will I see you next?" she asked in her best temptress voice.

Alex could almost read her mind. *Let's see now, one dinner, two rolls in the hay. Next, she'll be expecting me to divorce my wife and marry her.* He looked at the girl again. She was tall and curved in all the right places, and she was a great lay. *But baby, there are a million other girls out there, just like you.* "I have a surprise for you," he said.

The girl squealed and her face broke into a delirious smile. "Ohhh Alex! I love surprises."

He pulled a small box from his pocket and dropped it into her greedy hands. She opened the box and gasped. Inside, was a fine gold chain with a pendant in the shape of lips. "Oh Alex, you shouldn't have," she said again.

"It's an original by Fred. Here, let me help you put it on." He closed the clasp in the back of her neck and turned her around to face him. "They're not half as beautiful as your own lips, but then Fred never did get the pleasure of meeting you, did he?"

She giggled. "My lips can also do things these can't."

Alex gave her a bored little smile and waited impatiently for the driver to pull up in front of the girl's apartment building. "Listen baby, I'm going on a business trip, so you won't be hearing from me for awhile."

"Will you call me when you come back?" she asked, her eyes full of hope.

He leaned over and gave her a quick kiss on the mouth. "Just as soon as I can." He watched as she climbed out of the car and ran across the street to her building.

She fell for the 'Fred original' bit, Alex thought and chuckled. In reality, there were dozens of girls all over New York, all wearing identical pieces. *All members of the Alexander Ivanov blow-job club*, thought Alex with amusement.

A few years ago, Alex had seen the original piece in the window of Fred's and it had caught his fancy. On impulse, he had walked in and bought it with the intention of giving it to his girl of the moment. *Why spend that kind of money on someone I will only see two or three times?* he had asked himself later. Instead, he found a corner jeweler and convinced him to make a dozen copies of the piece. Since then, it had become a tradition for Alex. Whenever it was time to dump a girl, she got a pair of gold lips as a parting present. *I guess I'll have to run up another dozen copies soon*, he thought.

The blonde turned and waved, then walked into her building. Alex tapped on the window and the glass partition slid silently down. "Where to, Mr. A?" asked the driver, his face a mask if impassivity.

"Home, Ray. It's been a long day."

* * * * *

From her bedroom, Brigitte heard the loud crash across the hall, and she instinctively knew. "Réjeanne! *Viens vite!*" she yelled as she ran. "Hurry!" At the door of David's room, she stopped and listened for a moment. There was nothing but silence. "David!" she called out and knocked.

"What is it?" asked Réjeanne breathlessly as she came running up the stairs.

"I just heard a crash. I think..." She turned the handle and opened the door. Inside, David was thrashing about on the floor. Vomit was running from his mouth and he was making gurgling, choking sounds. "Quick," ordered Brigitte. "Help me turn him on his side."

She and Réjeanne pushed and pulled David's convulsing body until he lay on his side. Brigitte put her ear to his mouth and listened. "He's breathing clearly. I don't think he inhaled any vomit. Get me my kit."

Réjeanne ran out. A moment later she was back with a small leather bag. Brigitte grabbed it and pulled out the syringe. "Go get the car," she ordered. Réjeanne ran out again. With an experienced motion, Brigitte pulled up her son's sleeve and plunged the needle into his arm. A few minutes later, the seizures stopped. David's body relaxed, he opened his eyes and looked around, disoriented.

Brigitte was frantic. "Honey, we have to get you to the clinic." He looked at his mother blankly.

Réjeanne reappeared. "The car's ready," she said breathlessly.

"OK, he's ready. Is anyone around?"

"No. Jeremy was in the kitchen. I sent him to his room. I told him you wanted some privacy tonight."

"OK, let's go." The two women pulled David to his feet and with their arms under his shoulders, managed to half carry, half drag him all the way down the stairs, through the foyer, and outside to the car.

A moment later, Réjeanne watched as Brigitte's Mercedes pulled out with a squeal of tires. *I don't care how often I've seen him this way, it still kills me every time*, she thought to herself. The old woman turned to go back into the house when Alex's limousine drove up.

"Réjeanne, what are you doing out here this time of night?" Alex asked as he stepped out.

"Brigitte and David just left to go to dinner and I ran out to give Brigitte her bag. She had forgotten it on the credenza."

Alex grimaced. "They just left?" He looked at his watch. "For Chrissake, it's nearly midnight. Why would they want to go out at a time like this?"

• • • • •

The Bateman clinic was privately owned and operated. For years, David had been under the discreet care of Dr. Silver, a kindly old man with a shock of salt-and-pepper hair. He stepped out of David's room and joined Brigitte in the waiting area down the hall.

As soon as she saw him, Brigitte hurried over. "How is he?" she asked nervously.

"He's still post-ictal, so we've got him on IV. Good thing you gave him that shot of Valium. This attack was a bad one. He could have gone into another seizure immediately."

"Oh my God! Isn't that terribly dangerous?"

Dr. Silver hesitated for a moment. "It can be. So far we've been able to keep David's condition under very tight control, but I think we'll have to readjust his dosage again. I'm going to keep him in observation overnight. I'm sure, by morning, he'll be as good as new."

The relief was indescribable. Brigitte stammered a thank you and hurried to David's room. He was sleeping peacefully. She walked over and kissed his forehead. "Night sweetheart. I'll see you in the morning."

It was four a.m. when Brigitte finally got home. She tiptoed into the dark bedroom and slid carefully between the satin sheets. She stopped and listened. Alex's breathing was soft and regular. *Thank goodness I didn't wake him*, she thought, with relief.

"Where the hell have you been all night?" asked Alex suddenly in the dark.

Brigitte's heart nearly stopped. "Out," she answered, angrily.

There was a moment's hesitation before her husband continued. "Is that all the explanation you're going to give me?"

"That's right. That's the same explanation you give me all the time." She could feel his anger, but for once it didn't matter. "Oh, and by the way," she continued. "David will probably be late for work tomorrow."

"And why is that?"

"Let's just say, he's spending the night out."

To her surprise, she heard Alex chuckle. "That's a relief," he said. "I was beginning to worry about that boy. He's nearly twenty five and he still doesn't have a girlfriend."

The next morning, as soon as Alex had left for the office, Brigitte drove over to the clinic. She found David sitting up in bed and flirting with one of the nurses.

Brigitte laughed. "I guess I don't have to ask how you are," she said from the doorway.

The nurse blushed furiously and hurried out of the room.

"Now look what you've done," exclaimed David with a glint of amusement in his green eyes. "Just when I thought I might be getting somewhere with her."

Brigitte walked over and gave him a kiss on the cheek. "Sorry, sweetheart. I didn't mean to ruin your love life." She grew suddenly serious. "How are you this morning?"

"Fine. When do I get out of here?" he asked casually.

"Just as soon as the doctor allows it."

"And the doctor says he can leave right now," said Dr. Silver from the doorway. He walked into the room and sat at the foot of the bed. "I've changed your prescription David. Hopefully everything will be under control again. If you have any kind of episode again, no matter how minor, come back and see me right away." He got up from the bed and walked over to the door. "Oh, and by the way," he added with a smile. "Try not to flirt with my nurses. It gets them all silly and then they can't seem to get any work done for the rest of the day." He walked out.

Brigitte turned to David. "And what are you going to do for the rest of the day?"

"Go to the office," he replied as a matter of fact.

"Are you sure you should?"

"Absolutely. I feel fine."

Brigitte was not convinced, but on the way

back home, she dropped him off in front of Power Properties head office. "Take it easy David. Don't let Alex bulldoze you into working late."

"I won't. Don't worry." He leaned over and gave her a peck on the cheek. "Love you," he said as he stepped out of the car.

Brigitte watched her son run up the steps and disappear in the crowd. *I must be the luckiest woman in the world. I couldn't possibly have a more wonderful son.*

From her office, Natalia Berenson saw David hurry by. "Oh David!" she called out to him. David reappeared in the doorway. Natalia picked up a stack of drawings. "Are you going by Alex's office?"

"Yes, sure."

"Could you drop these on his desk for me?" she asked and handed him the pile.

"No problem."

"And by the way, I've been trying to get a hold of your mother this morning. Do you have any idea where she is?"

"She just dropped me off. I guess she'll be home in about forty-five minutes or so."

"Thanks, sweetheart." Natalia blew David a kiss and picked up the telephone. "Hello Réjeanne, it's me again. I think Brigitte forgot about our lunch date. Tell her we can do it tomorrow if she's free. Yes darling. The Russian Tea Room at one." Natalia put the telephone back down. *I hope I'm not making a mistake*, she thought morosely. *But I just can't stand by any longer and say nothing.*

● ● ● ● ●

CHAPTER 14

The Russian Tea Room was packed, as it always is at lunch time. Natalia walked in wearing her usual double layers of false lashes, her painted on eyebrows and heavily teased platinum hairdo. As soon as he saw her, the Maitre'D ran over. "Miss Berenson, how wonderful to see you again. You look absolutely gorgeous."

"Thank you, Peter. It's nice to see you too. I'm meeting Brigitte Ivanov for lunch. Is she here yet?"

"Not yet, but if you'll follow me, I'll take you right to your table."

Along the way, Natalia could hear the rumble of interest her arrival was causing. *Even thirty years and seventy pounds after my last movie, I can still make an entrance*, she thought with satisfaction. "Thank you Peter," she said when she was seated.

A few minutes later, Brigitte arrived, causing another flurry of attention. She kissed Natalia on both cheeks and rushed into her apology. "I'm so sorry about yesterday. I don't know where my mind was."

"Don't worry about it. I had so much work to do at the office. Today was much better for me." She picked up the menu and scanned it quickly. "I don't know about you, but I just love the blinis here."

"Perfect. That's what I'll have too." Brigitte closed her menu. A waiter hurried over and took their orders.

During the meal, the two women chatted about fashion and gossiped about the latest marriages and divorces among the jet set.

"You know what I find so strange," said Brigitte over coffee afterwards. "Is that Gerald has never remarried. I know he was very much in love with his wife, but he's been a widower for nearly twenty years now, and as far I can tell, half the female population in this city would be more than willing to have him."

"I know," said Natalia. "Unfortunately he's in love with a married woman."

Brigitte hesitated. "Is it anyone I know?" The thought of Gerald having an affair with a married woman, disturbed her. It was too sordid a behavior for Gerald.

"I'm really not at liberty to tell, Brigitte." She paused for a moment. She began to say something and stopped.

Brigitte leaned forward, her eyes full of concern. "Natalia, is there something wrong? You seem worried about something."

Natalia waited for a moment, and then took a deep breath and plunged in. "There is something bothering me, and I don't know what to do about it." She waited again before continuing. "I have a friend whose husband is…let's just say he is not very loyal. Normally, I would never interfere, but in this case, I believe this friend is unhappily married. Her husband is also very indiscreet. So many people are aware of the situation that it's just a matter of time before the newspapers get a hold of the story."

"Oh my God! You have to tell her."

Natalia sighed. "You have no idea how many times I've wanted to. But I really don't know if I should. She's so much in love with him. Maybe she's better off not knowing. I also have to consider the possibly that she might turn against me and hate me forever."

Brigitte shook her head vehemently. "No! You must tell her. I cannot imagine how I would feel if everyone knew Alex was having an affair and nobody had bothered to tell me. I think it would be so much worse. It would be..." She searched for words for a moment. "It would feel like a double betrayal. Natalia, you must tell her."

Natalia nodded and took a deep breath. "Brigitte," she said, her voice full of compassion. "That friend is you."

For a moment Brigitte stared at her blankly. "Wh-what?"

Natalia's eyes filled with tears. "I'm so sorry Brigitte. I really didn't know how else to tell you."

Brigitte's head was spinning. *No, this is not real. It cannot be.* Nevertheless, she knew that it was. It explained everything.

Natalia continued. "Maybe I shouldn't have said anything. Maybe I'm wrong. I could be making a mistake."

Brigitte's voice was calm. "No. You're not wrong. I know it's the truth."

Both women were silent for a moment. "What are you going to do?" asked Natalia.

For a long time, Brigitte could not answer. "I don't know," she said sadly. "I really don't know."

For days Brigitte was in a state of shock. She went about her usual routine, giving orders to the staff, preparing menus for the cook, making sure Alex's favorite meals were cooked, and accepting invitations to all the important functions in the city. Never in her life had she felt so unhappy. *What should I do? Please God, tell me what should I do.*

One moment, she wanted to leave her husband and never see him again. The next, she wanted to go on pretending everything was fine while she tried to find some way of making him fall in love with her again.

Oddly, it was Gerald Masson's advice she most wanted. *If only I could confide in him. I know he would tell me what to do. That is a stupid idea. I have to decide this on my own.* But try as she might, she could not. In the end, she decided, to not decide. *I am still too emotional. The worst thing I could do is decide impulsively. I don't want to have regrets later.*

So Brigitte said nothing, and watched in silent agony as Alex went about his usual routine.

* * * * *

They were sitting at breakfast. Brigitte nibbled half heartedly at a piece of toast as Alex made plans for David's upcoming twenty-fifth birthday.

"Let's have a party," he said between mouthfuls of scrambled eggs. "We can have it around the swimming pool. We'll cook steaks on the barbecue and put up an ice cream stand at one end of the pool and an open bar at the other. What do you think David?" As usual, he didn't wait for his stepson's answer and just continued making all the plans. "We'll invite the Carsons and the Steinbergs and the Fords."

"I thought the party was supposed to be for David," said Brigitte softly.

Alex looked at her exasperated. "If it's good for Power Properties, it's good for David," he answered sharply. "Don't you agree, David?"

"Yes, of course," answered David quietly.

Alex looked at Brigitte, his eyes full of scorn.

"Don't worry about any of the details. I'll take care of it myself." He threw his napkin on the table. "How about a swim in the pool, David. I could use the exercise." Without waiting for David's reply, he stormed off in a huff.

David walked around the table and put his arms around Brigitte. "Don't worry, mom. I really don't care about parties anyhow." He kissed her gently on the cheek and hurried off to get into his swimming trunks.

"You look tired David. Are you all right?"

"Hey! I'm not the one losing weight lately," he answered with a concerned smile. "Why don't you join us in the pool? Come, it'll be fun."

"Thanks sweetheart. You go ahead. I'll just go and rest upstairs." Brigitte waved him off and a moment later she heard him run out the back door. *When will this all end?* she thought. *I am just so exhausted. I don't think I can keep up this pretense much longer.* She pushed away her plate and went upstairs.

She sat on the bed and listened to the sounds of joyful splashing from the swimming pool. *I can't go on avoiding it forever.* The telephone rang, interrupting her thoughts, and she picked it up. "Oh hi, Natalia. Thank you, I'm fine. You don't have to worry about me." In the background she could hear Alex laughing. *How can he be so happy when I'm hurting so much?* She tried to concentrate on what Natalia was saying. "No, I haven't made up my mind about anything yet. I'm really not sure what I want to do." Suddenly, she became aware of the silence. The splashing in the pool had stopped.

She could hear Alex's through the closed window. "David," he was yelling. "If this is your idea of a joke it isn't funny."

"Natalia can you hold on for a second?" She put the receiver down and walked over to the window.

In the pool below, David was underwater, convulsing violently. Alex was standing on the side, yelling angrily. "David, that's enough. I want you to get out right this minute!" Slowly, the convulsions stopped and David remained motionless in the bottom of the pool.

Suddenly Brigitte heard someone screaming. The sound was a long loud howl, like that of an animal in pain. The sound went on, and on, and on. She had no idea that it came from her own throat.

• • • • •

Chapter 15

Often, in the evenings, when he studied for hours, trying to cram all that knowledge into his mind, Anne Turner's son would think of that other boy, David, and the easy life he was living. *There is no justice in this world*, he thought bitterly. *If there really was any justice, I would be living that life, and I would be vice-president of Power Properties.*

But the young man had a plan. It might take years, and a lot of luck, but then, as his mother often said. 'Luck is something you make.' *She's right. I'll make my own luck*, he would think then. *I don't want a handout. I'll earn every dollar I get.* And he would return to his studying with a vengeance.

CHAPTER 16

Alex stood by the side of the pool and felt his blood run cold. This joke was not funny. "That's enough David," he yelled once again, but with less conviction. But David remained motionless under the water. Slowly, the horrible realization dawned on Alex. This was no joke. Something was terribly, terribly wrong. With a burst of panic, he dove into the water and grabbed hold of David's bathing suit. He struggled to the surface and tried to keep David's head afloat while he yelled for help.

Seconds later, Réjeanne appeared from the breakfast room. For a moment, she watched in disbelief the scene before her.

"Help me!" yelled Alex again as he clung to the

edge. There was desperation in his voice. "Help me get him out."

Réjeanne hurried to the pool as fast as her old legs would carry her. Together, she and Alex managed to pull David's limp body onto the deck and Alex frantically began mouth to mouth resuscitation. "Call an ambulance," he ordered sharply between breaths and the old woman tottered away.

After what seemed like an eternity, the ambulance arrived. The attendants rushed to the poolside with their life-saving equipment. Then everything began to move at a reassuringly fast pace. In a matter of minutes, David was hooked up to the heart monitor. *Everything will be all right*, thought Alex.

"There's no heart rate," called out one attendant.

The second paramedic placed two paddles on David's chest. "Defibrillator's ready. One, two, three, go!" On 'go', a current of electricity jolted through David's body. The line on the heart monitor remained flat.

"Still no response," called out the first technician. "Give him 1 milligram of Epinephrine and 100 milligrams of Lidocain."

The second technician gave him the injection and placed the paddles on David's chest again. "One, two, three, go!" David's body arched, and fell to the ground again. The line on the heart monitor did not move.

For nearly an hour, the paramedics worked. A short distance away, the cook and the maids had gathered and watched in stunned silence. Réjeanne, tears running down her worn cheeks, tried to absorb all that was going on. *This can't be*, she thought. *It's all just a nightmare. I'll close my eyes and when I open them, everything will be all right.*

Alex stayed close to David and pleaded quietly. *Come on David, you can do it. Breathe damn it! Breathe!*

Finally, the senior of the two emergency workers took Alex aside. "I'm sorry Mr. Ivanov. There's nothing more we can do." Solemnly, they strapped David's body to a stretcher and took him away.

* * * * *

For the entire time, Brigitte stayed by the window starring at the pool below, an expression of pain and horror on her face. That was how Réjeanne found her after the ambulance had left.

"Brigitte, *ma pauvre chérie*," cried the old woman, as she hobbled into the bedroom, tears running down her wrinkled face. Her entire body was shaking with sobs. "I'm so sorry. I loved him like my own son." Réjeanne put her arms around Brigitte. "I can't believe it. I don't want to believe it."

There was something eerie about the way Brigitte remained motionless. Réjeanne pulled away. "Brigitte! Please, say something." Still Brigitte did not move. Réjeanne saw the frozen expression of horror on Brigitte's face, and for the second time that day she knew that something was terribly wrong.

· · · · ·

The doctor, a slender young man with a thick bushy mustache, arrived and examined Brigitte. She was sitting in an arm chair, where Réjeanne and Alex had placed her, the same frozen expression of horror on her face.

Doctor Sharp talked to himself as he noted the symptoms. "Accelerated heart rate... profusion of sweating... contracted muscles... This woman is in severe shock," he said. "How long has she been that way?" he asked as he pulled out a small flashlight and directed the beam into Brigitte's dilated pupils.

"Probably about two hours," Alex answered. "Her son drowned this morning, in the swimming pool below. Everybody was in such a panic; we didn't notice right away that she wasn't around. I think she saw the whole thing through the window." His voice was barely under control. In the last few hours, he felt as though he had aged a hundred years.

The doctor put away his flashlight. He lifted one of Brigitte's arms above her head and let go of it. Her arm stayed up. He gently placed her arm back down by her side. "It's called catatonic shock," he said as he pulled out a syringe. He gave her an injection and continued. "I'm afraid she'll have to be hospitalized."

"How long will she be that way?" asked Alex, frantic.

The doctor shook his head. "There no way that can be predicted. A catatonic shock occurs when a person witnesses something too horrible for their mind to accept. Their brain just shuts down. The symptoms rarely continue beyond a few days, but there have been cases where they can slip from shock and go into catatonic depression. Your wife is completely nonresponsive. She needs to be medicated and put on intravenous feeding."

Alex kneeled in front of his wife. "Brigitte, it's me. Sweetheart, look at me. Say something." Brigitte sat motionless in the chair, her mind frozen on a moment of indescribable horror.

"I'm sorry Mr. Ivanov, she can't hear you right now," said the doctor, gently. "She's completely unaware of anything around her." He hesitated. "I'll have to call an ambulance."

Alex nodded, helplessly. He felt completely drained.

For the second time that day, an ambulance came and left with someone he loved.

Real despair did not hit Alex until later that evening. He was in the library with Natalia, Andrew and Gerald who had hurried over as soon as they had heard.

"There's just so much to do," explained Alex. I don't know where to begin."

"You have Brigitte to think about right now," said Andrew. "You don't have to worry about anything else. We can take care of the arrangements for David's funeral."

Funeral! The word struck Alex like a physical blow. "I want him to have the most expensive casket that exists," he said, his voice trembling. "And Brigitte would want him to wear one of his Valentino suits."

"Don't worry Alex. I'll take care of it," said Natalia.

Gerald cleared his throat. "Alex, I've made a few discreet inquiries and I've found a private clinic I feel would be better equipped to take care of Brigitte. I don't like the idea of her being in a psychiatric ward."

"I'll make the decisions regarding my wife, if you don't mind," answered Alex sharply.

"Have you thought about David's obituary?" asked Natalia. "There are the newspapers to contact, services to arrange..."

Alex looked at her blankly, and suddenly his whole body was wracked with sobs. "I thought he was just fooling around. I had no idea he had epilepsy. If only I'd known..." His advisors looked on in disbelief as the head of Power Industries dissolved into a shaking, sobbing mess.

* * * * *

Alex had Brigitte transferred to a private clinic in Connecticut. The building was set on acres of beautiful grounds with majestic trees and flower gardens. The bedrooms were pleasantly decorated with floral wallpaper and coordinating balloon curtains on the windows. Schubert played softly from a central sound system and patients had twenty-four hour private nurses. Still, Alex was not satisfied. The next day, he placed calls all over the world and flew in the top psychiatrists from France, Switzerland and Germany.

After thoroughly examining the patient, the doctors concurred. "Severe catatonic shock," said Doctor Lemieux from France.

"I already knew that. The question is; will she get better?" asked Alex, dreading the answer.

"It's hard to say," replied Doctor Shumaker from Germany. "Sometimes, a patient can make a complete recovery, but sometimes they remain in a semi-responsive state for years."

"Isn't there anything that can be done?" asked Alex. "I'm a wealthy man. Whatever she needs... Surely, something can be done."

"Arrangements have been made to start ECT tomorrow," said doctor Lemieux.

"ECT. What's that?"

"Electroshock treatment," replied doctor Moreland from Switzerland. "Under these circumstances, it is our best recourse."

Alex gasped. "Electroshock treatment! I thought those went out with the dark ages."

"Not at all! The treatment is still very common, and very effective I might add. There is no danger whatsoever, and the patient feels no pain," doctor Lemieux explained patiently. "There are three different kinds of catatonia. There is schizophrenic catatonia which occurs when a schizophrenic patient becomes completely disassociated. That is not the case here. Nor is the second type, which occurs because of some form of pressure on the brain, mainly in the case of large tumors. What your wife has is hysterical catatonia, which is the type that responds best to ECT."

"How does the shock treatment work?" asked Alex, as nightmarish visions of Brigitte being electrocuted flashed through is mind.

"The ECT will transmit an electric current through her brain, sending her into unconsciousness. When she awakens spontaneously—that can be anywhere from a few minutes to half an hour after the treatment—there is a good chance that she will be fully conscious as soon as she opens her eyes."

Alex thought furiously. Brigitte had already been catatonic for over forty eight hours. "How many of these treatments would she need?"

"The average is usually between four and six."

"What about possible side effects?"

"She might feel slightly disoriented for a short time. She might even have some memory lapses, but generally those symptoms leave after a few days. Otherwise, she will be communicating, thinking and acting quite normally."

Still Alex hesitated. "Do-do you really think…"

"You have to understand one thing. Even though her shock is of a hysterical nature, it is just as dangerous as any other form of shock. Unless we can decelerate her heart rate, and relax her muscular tension, she could go into cardiac arrest. If that were my wife in there," said doctor Moreland sympathetically, "I wouldn't hesitate for one minute."

Alex slowly nodded, accepting it. Then dully, "Fine, do whatever you have to do."

"We'll need you to sign some forms."

"I'll sign them. Just do it."

After signing the necessary papers, Alex

hurried back to Brigitte's room. The nurse looked up from her reading. "Good evening Mr. Ivanov."

Nothing good about it, thought Alex. "Any changes?" he asked, still hoping that the ECT would not be necessary.

The nurse shook her head sadly. "No, no changes whatsoever." She picked up her book and left discreetly. Alex sat by Brigitte's bed. He held her hand and listened to the sound of her breathing, in and out, slow and regular. He closed his eyes and pretended that she was only sleeping. But when he looked at her, she stared straight ahead, her face the same mask of pain and horror.

God why? he asked. But he knew the answer. *This is my punishment for all the times I've cheated on her.* God had decided that he did not deserve to have a wife and a son, and now He had taken both away from him.

Alex was not a praying man, but he tried to bargain with God. *Please, if you save her, I'll do anything.*

Then he denied God. *If there really was a God, He wouldn't punish the innocent. What kind of a God would kill off a brilliant young man with his whole life ahead of him? What kind of a God would make a mother witness such a horror?*

In the end Alex accepted that this was one situation in which he had no power whatsoever. He had never felt so helpless in his life.

Hours later, Alex was awakened by the apologetic nurse. "I'm sorry Mr. Ivanov. You fell asleep. There's nothing more you can do here..."

"It's all right. I was just leaving." He struggled out of his chair and left. *There's nothing more I can do.*

The following day, at three o'clock in the afternoon, the visitors were ushered out of the funeral parlor and the director prepared to close the coffin.

"Wait!" Alex stepped forward. "I want to be alone with him for a moment. The director nodded, understanding, and left. Alex looked down into the coffin. David looked so young, so peaceful. *He's only twenty four.* Alex leaned over and kissed him. *This is for your mother.* Then he turned and walked out. Outside the door, he nodded to the funeral director. "You can go ahead, now."

• • • • •

At three thirty, Brigitte was strapped to a table. Two electrodes were placed on her temples, and an injection of Celucurine, 45 mg, and Brevatonal 4 mg, was administered to paralyze her muscles, prevent them from contracting during the ECT.

Doctor Lemieux checked the dials, pushed the switch and Brigitte's body stiffened.

At that same moment, miles away, David's body was rolled into the mouth of the crematorium.

* * * * *

After the ceremony, Alex rushed back to the clinic with an enormous basket full of pink roses. Maybe, just maybe, Brigitte would be better. He walked into Brigitte's room and the young nurse greeted him with a smile. "Good evening Mr. Ivanov," she said. It was the first time he had seen her look so cheerful.

"I don't know," he said. "Is it really a good evening?"

She nodded and smiled. "Indeed it is. Mrs. Ivanov is sleeping now, but she was awake for a few minutes ago."

Alex spent the night in the armchair next to Brigitte's bed. It was such a relief to see Brigitte sleeping peacefully. Her face was relaxed, the expression of pain gone. He looked at her and wondered at his own stupidity. *How could I have been such a fool? I love her. I always have. I swear I'll make it up to you, my darling.*

In the small hours of the morning, he fell asleep. When he woke up, the sun was shining through the window and Brigitte was looking at him.

"Sweetheart! I'm..." Alex started to speak but the look in Brigitte eyes stopped him. *It's like she's looking at a stranger*, he thought. "Brigitte? Sweetheart, can you hear me?" There was no response. Brigitte was not looking at him, she was looking through him. Alex felt sick to his stomach. He rushed out of the room.

At the reception, the secretary was busy filing charts. "I want to see doctor Lemieux," Alex demanded. He looked ready to kill.

"Right away sir," she answered and picked up the intercom. "Doctor Lemieux, come to reception, please. Doctor Lemieux." Her voice echoed through the clinic.

A moment later, the doctor hurried down the hall. "Mr. Ivanov," he greeted him cheerily. "I have some very good news."

Alex was livid. "I just saw my wife. She looked right at me and she didn't even recognize me."

The doctor smiled benignly. "She is doing very well. The catatonia has receded considerably. This was just the first treatment and she is already responding..."

"She did not recognize me!" shouted Alex. He was frantic. "How can you stand there and tell me she's doing better?"

"Come with me," said the doctor. He guided Alex down the hall to a small office. "Please forgive the mess. Since I am not regular staff, this is the best the clinic could provide me with. Would you like a drink? Scotch? Gin?"

"Scotch," said Alex weakly.

"As I was saying," continued Lemieux gently, as he handed Alex the drink. "You wife is doing very well." He saw the doubt in Alex's eyes and kept talking. "This was only the first treatment and she is responding beautifully. Her heart rate is normal, her sweating has disappeared. She is even responding to pain."

"Did-did she feel..."

"The electroshock?" the doctor completed the question for Alex. "No, of course not. Only the needle test. We pricked her lightly when she regained consciousness and she responded. That is not to say that she is cured. Her condition is simply not as severe. She will still need further ECTs, just as we had anticipated."

Alex listened to everything the doctor had to say. But he did not feel any better. *She looked right through me*, he kept thinking. *As if I was a complete stranger.*

Over the following weeks, Brigitte was given six more ECTs. After each treatment, her condition improved slightly. After the last session, the doctor asked for a meeting with Alex. "Your wife is no longer catatonic but there is still an emotional block of some sort. Although she is completely aware of her surroundings, she refuses to respond. It is almost as though she doesn't want to recover. In order for me to be able to help her any further, I need to know what she is repressing. I don't think giving her any more ECTs is the answer. I suggest trying sodium amytal."

"Sodium amytal, isn't that some kind of truth serum?" asked Alex, worried.

"That is the popular misconception. Under the influence of sodium amytal, your wife will simply be dis-inhibited. I am convinced that there has to be something more than just seeing her son drown. Guilt, rage, some emotion so powerful she is afraid of allowing herself to feel it. Whatever that emotion is, the knowledge of it will give me the information I need to help her. Without that knowledge, it could take months, years of therapy before we find the answer."

Alex sighed. "Where do I sign?"

* * * * *

Chapter 17

A few days later, the sodium amytal treatment was administered. Doctor Lemieux sat by Brigitte's bed and spoke softly. "There is nothing to worry about. This is just a small injection to help you relax." He pushed the needle into Brigitte's arm. He waited for a few minutes and began to speak slowly and gently. "Brigitte, I am going to ask you to listen very carefully. I want you to answer my questions as honestly as you can. Will you do that for me?"

Slowly, Brigitte nodded. Her eyes were closed. As long as she was sleeping, all of it was just a nightmare. So Brigitte continued the game with herself. She would continue sleeping, because she knew that if she woke up, David would be dead.

It was all her fault. She had tried to kill him when he was still in her womb. She had lied about his condition and allowed him to go swimming. As long as she was sleeping, David was there with her. *Hi mom. Did you see my painting? Can we put it up in the library?*

* * * * *

Over the next few months, Alex felt like he was on a giant treadmill. Although Brigitte was improving, the progress was slow. Every week he drove out to the clinic to see her. During those visits he talked, and for the most part she seemed to hear him, but she never spoke, or smiled, or even looked at him.

"She is consumed with guilt over her son's death," explained the doctor.

"But that's ridiculous," said Alex. "She wasn't even near the pool. There was nothing she could have done. If anything, she should blame me."

"When she was pregnant with David, she attempted to perform an abortion on herself. That guilt, combined with the fact that she hid his true condition from you during all those years, are the reasons she blames herself for his death. She's being treated with antidepressants, and I'm continuing her therapy." He tried to sound convincing. "I have every reason to believe that she will get better."

She must get better. What would I do without her? Over the last few months, he had come to realize how much he depended on her. During all the years of their marriage, she had always been there for him, supporting him, encouraging him and always believing in him. Brigitte was more than his wife. She was his best friend. *Why did I need all those other women?* he often thought. *I had the most loving woman in the world right there waiting for me.*

As if Alex's worries about Brigitte were not enough, for the first time since the birth of Power Properties, the company was experiencing financial difficulties.

The directors were gathered in the conference room.

"How can we be in this situation?" asked Alex, as he pored over the financial statements.

"It's really very simple," explained Gerald. "We are overextended. The cost of renovating the

Royal Victoria was three times more than what we budgeted for. We've had to contend with labor strikes, increases in the cost of materials, and we are still facing endless delays. Every time we turn around there's some new problem. No matter how soon we finish the project, we can't possibly make it profitable for at least five to seven years."

"What about the casinos in Atlantic city?"

"The first casino was remortgaged to pay for the building of the second, and the second casino was remortgaged to pay for the Royal Victoria," said Natalia. "Although they are both grossing more than any other casino in the country, all the money goes for the mortgages and the costs of operation. Not only is there nothing left over, but we're falling behind in the payments."

Andrew spoke. "I've been looking for possible buyers... "

"I don't want to sell," interrupted Alex. "Every one of those projects is a gold mine. All we need is time. I'll talk to the bank myself," said Alex. "They've been doing business with Power Properties for years. I'm sure they'll allow us an extension."

Andrew shook his head. "Alex, be reasonable. We could liquidate a few..."

"You are either with me, or against me! Is that clear?" Alex was livid. He glared at Andrew.

Andrew stared back. "Perfectly," he answered icily.

Natalia spoke, breaking the tension. "Alex, Andrew did not mean to sound disapproving. We've all been under a lot of pressure these last few months. And Andrew has been taking most of it."

Alex nodded glumly. "Now, as far as the bank is concerned, let me take care of it."

After the meeting, Gerald waited for Alex in the hallway. "How's Brigitte?" he asked. "Is she responding to her treatments?"

"She's fine," answered Alex abruptly. "Don't worry about my wife. She's getting the best care available."

Gerald nodded quietly and walked away.

The next day, Alex went to see the First Country bank. The president, a wiry old man with eyes like steel, ushered him into his office and Alex opened his briefcase. Alex took out the company's statements and projections of earnings and spread them before the man.

"As you can see," Alex explained. "This difficulty is only temporary. All we need is time. In a few months, the Power Hotel and Casino will be fully paid off, and that will alleviate our debt load considerably. After that point, we will have no trouble meeting our payments."

"I understand your position, Mr. Ivanov. But you must also understand ours," said Sidney Elmsby, stiffly. "You owe this bank nearly one billion dollars. And you are in default on your payments. That puts us in a very shaky position. When you started falling behind on your payments, I took the initiative of looking into your company. Now I find that the figures you gave us were grossly inflated. Your properties are not worth nearly as much as you reported." He pulled out a folder and began to read. "According to our independent real estate evaluator, the Power Properties Tower Hotel and Casino is worth—"

"...is worth whatever I can get for it," said Alex confidently. "And I have an Arabian sheik who is willing to buy it for double the amount of your estimate."

The president hesitated. "Are you absolutely sure about that?"

"Would you like to speak to him? I also have a buyer for the Royal Victoria."

The president held his breath for a moment. Maybe he was being paranoid. After all, Ivanov did have a point. An evaluation was, after all, only an opinion. A property was worth as much as anyone was willing to pay for it. If Ivanov had a potential buyer lined up, then... "I would like to speak to him," he said tersely.

Alex picked up the telephone. "Would you mind placing a call for me?" he asked pleasantly. He gave the overseas number and waited until a foreign voice answered on the speaker phone.

"This is Alex Ivanov. May I speak to Sheik Omar El Kayem please?" As he spoke, Alex noticed the sudden relief on Elmsby's face as he recognized sheik El Kayem's name. Just a few weeks ago, the *New York Times* had published an extensive article about the sheik, in which they described him as being the Arab-world's richest man. The article had gone on to list his toys—the most expensive private yacht ever built, a multimillion dollar helicopter, palaces all over Europe, and the sheik's greatest pride and joy, the most extensive private collection of grand masters in the world.

Minutes later, Sheik El Kayem was on the line. "Alex! How are you my friend? So do we have a deal?'

"Omar," Alex said agreeably into the receiver. "I've been thinking about your offer, and it sounds interesting. I just wanted to clarify one detail before I take it to my board of directors. The amount you quoted for the Royal Victoria, was that in Swiss Francs or in American dollars?"

"Very nice try, my friend," came the amused reply. "That was one billion American dollars and not one penny more."

"Thanks Omar. I'll have an answer for you in a few days."

After the call was ended, the president nodded, reassured. "You must understand," he said, apologetically. "So many companies are having difficulties. One can never be too careful."

"I understand," said Alex agreeably as he stood to leave.

Later that afternoon, Alex went back to his office and placed a call to Saudi Arabia. "Omar, you'll be getting the three paintings tomorrow."

"I am very grateful my friend. It is always good to do business with you. I've had my heart set on those paintings for a long time. The money will be wired to your account as soon as I verify their authenticity. If you ever need my help again, I will be happy to cooperate."

The next day, Alex went for his weekly visit to the clinic. At the entrance, the doctor rushed to greet him. "I have wonderful news," he exclaimed. "Brigitte has asked to see you."

Alex hurried to Brigitte's room. At the door, he suddenly hesitated. What if she looked at him with that blank stare again? What if she didn't recognize him? He opened the door, and walked in.

Brigitte was sitting by the window. She turned, looked at him and smiled. It was the most beautiful sight Alex had ever seen. "Hi," he said. His hands were trembling.

"How are you Alex?"

Alex stumbled to the chair, kneeled and put his arms around her. "I've missed you," he said, his voice close to breaking.

"Did you?"

There was so much he wanted to say. "Brigitte, I'm so sorry about David. It was my fault. I thought..."

Brigitte closed her eyes, but not quickly enough to hide the flash of pain. "It was an accident. Nobody's fault. Just a terrible accident."

Relief flooded over him and he was filled with overwhelming joy. Everything would be all right. "God, I love you!" he said, and was amazed at how profoundly he meant it.

At the end of the visit, as Alex was about to leave, Brigitte put a restraining hand on his arm. "I-I want you to do me a favor," she said.

"Anything."

"Could you ask Natalia to come and see me?" she asked. "I would appreciate it."

"I'll call her right away, sweetheart."

The next day, Natalia arrived at the clinic. For months she had been filled with guilt. If only she had not told Brigitte about Alex's infidelities, maybe she would not have had such a severe reaction to her son's death a few weeks later. As it was, Brigitte had been dealt two severe emotional blows in a very short time. Since then, Natalia had often wanted to visit Brigitte, but had dreaded her friend's reaction. At the door to Brigitte's room she gathered her courage and walked in. "How are you, darling?" she asked, rushing over to embrace her.

"Natalia, I'm so glad you came," responded Brigitte quietly. There was no anger in her voice, no sign of distress or sorrow. If Brigitte held any grudge toward Natalia, there was no sign of it.

"Of course, I came as soon as Alex told me," said Natalia, relieved. "I wanted to come much sooner but I..." She gestured vaguely. "...wasn't sure you would want to see me." She sat in the armchair and held on to Brigitte's hands as she spoke. "Gerald sends his best."

"That's nice of him." Brigitte hesitated. "I want to ask you a favor."

Natalia nodded and her triple chins wobbled like jelly. "Anything Brigitte. You have my word."

Brigitte struggled to speak for a moment and her eyes filled with tears. "Did you ever tell Alex about what you told me?"

For a moment, Natalia almost lost her composure, but she quickly regained it. She shook her head. "No."

"I want you to promise me you never will. As far as I am concerned, Alex is my husband and he has never even looked at another woman. Do you promise?"

Natalia was at a loss. This was not what she had expected. "Yes, of course. Anything you say."

"Thanks Natalia. I'm very tired now. If you don't mind, I think I'd like to sleep. Don't worry, I'm all right."

As Natalia left, she couldn't help but think that Brigitte did not sound all right at all.

* * * * *

A few days later, Doctor Lemieux gave Alex the good news. "I think Brigitte is nearly ready to go home. You'll be able to bring her home for Christmas."

Alex took the news ecstatically and rushed home to prepare for his wife's impending arrival. Alex walked through the rooms, trying to think of ways to make the house more beautiful for the upcoming holidays and his wife's homecoming. Everywhere he looked, were reminders of David. Memories, some happy, some sad, filled his mind. *This is where David used to paint*, he thought as he stood in the solarium. He walked into the library and looked at David's painting of the sunset. *He really did have talent*, he thought. *And he was so proud of this painting.* Upstairs in his bedroom, David's clothes still hung in the closets. His favorite books were neatly lined in the shelves across from his bed, and the oils he had painted years ago decorated the walls. *It's as though he was still here.*

Alex walked dejectedly through the rest of the house. Everywhere he looked there was something to remind him of David. *If it's this painful for me to be reminded of him, it will be torture for Brigitte.*

At that moment, Alex knew exactly what he should do. "Réjeanne!" he called. The old woman appeared, wiping her hands on her apron. "I want you to get rid of all of David's things."

Réjeanne's mouth dropped open. "B-but" She was stuttering.

"No buts about it. Just do it. Brigitte will be back in a few weeks and I don't want her to be reminded of David everywhere she looks."

• • • • •

One month later, Brigitte was discharged from the clinic. Doctor Lemieux walked her to the car, giving her last minute advice. "I have to go back to France, but I want you to continue seeing a therapist twice a week. Here is his name and telephone number. And don't forget to take your medication."

"I won't," she replied. She felt like a schoolgirl at graduation: happy, sad, and frightened.

Alex helped her into the limousine, and then climbed in the other side.

An hour later, the car pulled into the long circular drive. The chauffeur stepped out and opened the door for Brigitte. With the snow on the ground, and the Christmas decorations, the house looked like a magical holiday scene. *How can it be Christmas without David*, thought Brigitte, sadly.

Alex opened the massive front door and escorted her inside. "Would you like something to eat?" he asked as he put her suitcases down in the front foyer. "Or would you rather go straight to our bedroom and rest?"

"I think I'd like to be alone," she answered hesitantly. "You go. I'll just wander around by myself."

"Maybe that's not such a good idea."

"Alex, I want to be alone." Her tone was firm.

"If you're sure, I'll be upstairs in our bedroom," he said. "If you need anything..."

Brigitte wasn't sure what she had expected, but whatever it was, this was not it. *I know David is gone*, she thought, still unable to even think the word 'dead'. *But where are all his things?* With growing trepidation, Brigitte walked through the rooms. Everything was slightly different. There were new pictures on the grand piano in the living room. In the library, she stood shocked. David's painting of the sunset was gone. In its place was a new Matisse. *No, it can't be.* She turned and ran. At the door to David's bedroom, she hesitated. *I'll open the door and he'll be there.* She closed her eyes and walked in.

For a moment she thought she had made a mistake. *This isn't David's room.* All of the furniture had been changed. She rushed to the closets. *His clothes are gone.* In the bathroom she stared at the empty counters. *All his colognes, gone.* She would have given anything for just the familiar smell of his aftershave. She opened the cabinet. Nothing. Every last trace of David was gone, vanished! It was as though his very memory had been obliterated. *He's gone*, she thought. All hopes of the past months having been a nightmare, crumpled. *My son is gone, and he's never coming back.* At last the tears came, hot and salty and bitter. *David!* she cried. *Oh God David, where are you!*

. . . . .

CHAPTER 18

The newspaper had yellowed in the months since it had been published. Anne Turner pulled it out gingerly from the box where she had stored it, and spread it on the table.

TRAGEDY STRIKES IVANOV FAMILY

Anne Turner smiled as she remembered the day she had first read the article.

In her excitement, she had almost stumbled on her way to the telephone. She had dialed quickly and willed her son to be there.

"Come on, dammit. Pick up the telephone." She heard the voice at the other end, sleepy and confused. *"It's me. Did you read this morning's paper?"*

"What time is it?" he had asked still groggy.

"What the hell were you doing last night? I sold the house and all of my jewelry to send you to Harvard, and you go out and party all night."

"I was not out. I was studying. My board exams are in just a few months and I have dozens of books to memorize. I'm tired."

"Well this will cheer you up." She read the article out loud, putting emphasis on a few more important words. *"'The adopted son of Alex Ivanov, who, many believed, was being groomed to take over his father's company, has died.' Did you get that?"*

"Yes, yes I got it." His voice had suddenly become wide awake.

"And get this. 'Apart from his wife, there is no other living relative.'"

Anne Turner remembered her son's shock after she finished reading him the article, and smiled. She folded up the old newspaper. *You are in for a big surprise Alex Ivanov.*

• • • • •

Chapter 19

Over dinner a few days later, Alex told Brigitte of his intentions. "From now on, I'm going to spend more time with you and less at the office. I missed you while you were away, sweetheart."

Brigitte looked at him blandly. "Why would you do that? You love working."

"But you've always wanted me to spend more time..."

Brigitte laughed weakly. "*Mon chéri*, I wouldn't know what to do with you if you suddenly had time for me. Maybe our marriage has been successful all these years because of our busy lives."

"Are you sure? I thought ..."

"Don't worry about me. I'm fine. I don't want anything to change from the way things were."

Alex was puzzled. In the past, Brigitte had used every opportunity to pressure him into spending more time with him. "If you're absolutely sure," he said.

"I am," she answered.

Alex nodded and smiled. "I bet you can't wait to get in contact with all your friends. By the way, Gerald sends his regards." He kept up a happy chatter, carefully covering the way he truly felt. *She's changed*.

· · · · ·

As Brigitte reentered her life after her release from the clinic, Alex was not the only one to notice the change in her. Whereas in the past, she had always been warm and approachable, Brigitte now seemed distant, aloof. When her friends, even Natalia, tried to draw her into conversations, more often than not, Brigitte seemed disinterested.

"Alex, I'm very worried about her," Natalia told him one day after Brigitte had refused still another invitation to join her for lunch.

"She still hasn't recovered from David's death," he answered.

But in reality it was more than that.

* * * * *

Every day, Brigitte went through the motions of living. She got up in the morning and dressed with the same care and attention she had always taken. She filled her days to overflowing with activities. She shopped, worked out at the gym, oversaw the decorating of the many Power Properties projects; she continued caring for the house and for Alex; but she no longer seemed to have any interest in spending time with anyone. There was only emptiness inside, and she desperately tried to fill it by rushing about in a constant whirlwind of activities.

After numerous attempts to draw her out, Natalia decided it was time to be more forceful. After work one day, she drove over to the Ivanov house unannounced. "How is she?" she asked Réjeanne as soon as the woman opened the door.

Réjeanne looked worried. "I don't know. She hardly talks to me anymore. She's always telling me she's too busy. She rushes around all the time, and if she's home, she just sits, staring off into space."

Natalia slipped out of her sable coat and handed it to Réjeanne. "Where is she?"

"In the library," she replied. "Should I tell her you're here?"

"No, it's all right. I'll tell her myself," and she strode determinedly across the foyer.

Brigitte was sitting quietly, staring absently at the fire in the chimney. She looked up. "Natalia, what a surprise..." She seemed confused. "I'm sorry. Did I forget you were coming?"

"Darling, I'm worried about you." Natalia walked over, kissed her on each cheek and settled her weight into one of the armchairs. "Every time I want to see you, you put me off. Gerald tells me he also left you countless messages and that you never returned his calls. Are you all right?"

Brigitte stood up wearily. "I'm fine. I'm just so busy lately. You should have told me you were coming over. I would have asked Jerome to prepare dinner."

Natalia shook a cigarette out of her platinum case and lit it. Slowly, she took a deep drag and exhaled, looking at Brigitte directly in the eyes.

"You would have done no such thing. You would have come up with some excuse to put me off again."

Brigitte seemed to deflate. "I-I'm sorry Natalia."

"I think I understand how you feel Brigitte, but it's time you came back to the living. A group of us are having lunch tomorrow at Lutèce and you are joining us." She saw Brigitte begin to shake her head and quickly continued, insisting. "And I am not taking no for an answer."

* * * * *

The next day, Brigitte was stepping out of her limousine in front of the restaurant when a group of reporters assailed her. 'Why did you disappear for so long?' they wanted to know. 'Is it true that you've had a nervous breakdown?' 'How are you feeling now?'

Struggling to remain calm while avoiding the barrage of questions, Brigitte escaped into the restaurant and was quickly escorted to the long table where most of her friends were already seated.

Natalia rose to greet her. "I'm sorry you had to

go through that. Someone must have tipped them off that you would be here."

Brigitte shook her head. "I should have expected it. You can't imagine how they've been hounding me since I've come home."

"I can imagine," replied Christina Albertini, the recently divorced socialite. "When George and I separated, the reporters were practically camped on my doorstep for weeks."

"And look at the way they turned the Bradley divorce into a circus," commented Gloria Steinberg. "That went on for over a year. It was an absolute disgrace."

The group ordered lunch and the conversation turned to the latest fashion. From across the table, Natalia watched with relief as Brigitte joined in the chatter. *This is exactly what Brigitte needed. It can only do her good to be out with friends again.*

"Are you going to Paris for the collections?"

"Absolutely. I wouldn't miss it for the world."

"Hemlines are going up again."

"Can you believe Chistian Lacroix's last collection?"

"I just loved the last Dior showing."

One young woman, a tall angular blonde with large feline eyes, who had lately graced the covers of *Vogue* and *Bazaar* leaned toward Brigitte and whispered discreetly, "That's a beautiful pendant you're wearing."

Brigitte looked down at the eighteen-carat gold lips hanging from the chain around her neck and smiled. "Thank you," she said. "My husband gave it to me for our wedding anniversary a few years ago." She looked at the blonde and suddenly noticed that she was wearing the identical piece. "You have the same necklace!"

"Yes," said the blonde with a smile that showed off two rows of perfect pearly whites, but did not quite reach her eyes. "But mine was a goodbye present. Alex is very generous man." She turned away, leaving Brigitte's imagination to interpret her comment.

After the meal, Brigitte pleaded a headache and hurried away from the table. Natalia watched as Brigitte rushed out of the restaurant. "What happened?" she asked the blonde.

"How would I know?" the cover girl replied coolly. "She hardly said two words to me during the entire meal."

* * * * *

In her bedroom, Brigitte tried to keep herself from thinking of what the blonde had said. But no matter how she tried, the words kept coming back to her. 'Mine was a goodbye present. Alex is a very generous man.' *That could not have meant... Or could it?* After a long time, she pulled herself off the bed and forced herself to go through Alex's drawers. *I have to know. Once and for all, I have to know.* Systematically, she ruffled through stack after stack of fine-linen shirts, luxurious cashmere sweaters. She went through his silk underwear and socks, checking the pockets of every jacket and every pair of pants in his room-size walk-in closet. She wasn't sure what she was looking for, only that whatever there was, she would find it.

She pulled out the shoe boxes from the top of the closet and threw them upside down on the floor. Suddenly she stopped. On the floor, amid the myriad of shoes that lay scattered around, were seven fine gold chains with pendants in the shape of lips. Brigitte picked up the last box she had thrown on the floor. Inside was the receipt from a jewelry store. Slowly, as if in a trance, she walked to the telephone and dialed the number of the store.

"Hello, I would like to place an order please," she said calmly into the receiver as her heart beat furiously inside her chest. "Who should I speak to?" For a moment she waited until the owner of the store came to the phone. "Yes, hello. My name is Leonora Hart. I am Alex Ivanov's private secretary. Mr. Ivanov would like you to run up another order of those necklaces for him. How long will that take? Oh, and before I forget. Mr. Ivanov would like to be reminded of how many of these orders he has placed the past." She paused again while the owner looked through his files. "Thank you very much," she replied when he gave her the information.

Brigitte was in shock. *Three dozen! My God!*

Then she ran to the toilet and threw up.

* * * * *

Gerald Masson was in a quandary. He sat in his office, two doors down from Alex's and drummed his fingers in a nervous staccato on his desk. Since Brigitte's discharge from the clinic, he fought a constant battle against his overwhelming need to see her. *I only want to see for myself that she's well. Nothing wrong with that.* He picked up the phone decisively and dialed.

"Hello," Brigitte answered after the third ring.

At the sound of her voice, relief washed through him. "Brigitte, I'm so glad you're there. I've been trying to reach you. How are you?"

"I-I'm fine." There was a tremor in her voice. "I'm sorry I didn't return your calls. I-I've been ..."

"You don't have to explain. I understand." Gerald was silent for a moment; a silence full of warmth and caring. "Brigitte, if you ever need me, I'm there for you."

There was another silence. "I-I need you," she said, and began to cry.

For a moment, Gerald thought his heart might stop. When he could trust his voice again, he answered. "I'm on my way."

"No! I don't want you to come here." There was desperation in her voice. "I'll meet you at your house."

Gerald rushed out of his office and was home in record time. Fifteen minutes later, he had changed into a fresh shirt and a pot of coffee was already brewing in the kitchen when the doorbell rang.

He opened the door and before he could say anything, Brigitte fell into his arms, her whole body wracked with sobs. His arms instinctively wrapped themselves around her. "What's wrong?" he asked, only to be answered with more tears. He could feel her breasts against his chest, her breath on his neck. He could smell her perfume. Involuntarily he felt himself become aroused. "I'm not sure this is wise," he whispered and pulled away.

Brigitte stood trembling before him. "Would you please make love to me?"

"Wh-what?" For a moment he thought he had misunderstood.

"Alex has had a string of women throughout our marriage. Our whole marriage is nothing but a farce. I can't stand him to even touch me anymore. Please... I want you to make love to me. I want to feel like a woman again."

He groaned.

"I'm sorry Brigitte. Believe me I want to make love to you more than anything in the world. But I can't, not under these circumstances."

"I-I don't understand. I'm asking you to. I want you to."

"I know." Then as if to himself, he said, "God this is hard."

"If you think I'll regret it, I won't," she said. "I should have divorced Alex years ago. I want a man who will love me, the way you loved your wife."

Before she would change her mind, Gerald pulled her into the doorway and closed the door behind her.

After the lovemaking, Brigitte lay contented with her head on Gerald's shoulder and her legs tangled with his. So this was what making love with Gerald felt like. There had been no fireworks, no earth shattering earthquakes—just a calm and natural feeling of wholeness. She sighed happily. She felt sated, like after a satisfying meal. She did no worry about not being good enough or about her body not pleasing him. His tenderness had spoken volumes. "I can hear your heart beating," she whispered.

Gerald's arms tightened around her. "No regrets?" he asked.

"No regrets." She smiled. "Tell me again that you love me."

"I fell in love with you the first time I met you. You looked so beautiful, and so lost. You waited all evening for Alex to show up and you were trying so hard to be patient. I remember thinking that, if you were my wife, I would never have let you go to that party by yourself."

Brigitte snuggled closer. "I was attracted to you too, but I was married. What else could I do?"

"And you're still married." He pulled away and looked at her. "What are we going to do about that?"

Brigitte hesitated. "I-I wish you and Alex were not partners. Is there any possibility you could leave the company?"

"It isn't that simple." He shook his head. "Everything I have is tied up in Power Properties, and right now, Alex is in no position to buy me out. He's overextended and cash poor."

"What about Natalia and Andrew?"

"They are in exactly the same position I'm in."

"Oh God! What a mess!"

"Don't worry. We'll think of something." He pulled her in his arms and covered her with kisses. "Now that I've got you, I won't ever let you go. I would kill, rather than risk losing you."

* * * * *

Brigitte and Alex ate in silence with the strains of Chopin playing softly in the background. The formal dining room seemed almost gloomy in the early evening light. Alex stole a glance at his wife. "How was your day?" he asked between bites of beef Wellington.

She shrugged. "Nothing special." She speared another asparagus, deftly cut a bite size piece and brought it to her mouth.

Alex searched her face for a clue. "What did you do all day?"

Brigitte kept her eyes on her plate. "What do you want Alex, a minute by minute playback?"

"I'm only trying to make conversation."

Brigitte sighed. "Sorry." She put down her fork and continued. "My life is so boring—shopping, lunches, just a lot of killing time. Why don't you tell me about your day? It has to be more interesting than mine. What are you working on lately?"

Alex hesitated. "I'm working on solving problems—nothing that would interest you."

She looked up, suddenly interested. "Problems? What kind of problems."

"Just the regular stuff. You know…cash flow."

"How bad is it?"

"It isn't bad. It's just that I have my eye on a piece of land and the board is against buying anything right now. We're a bit tight at the moment."

Brigitte pushed away her plate and looked up. "What piece of land is that?"

"In Atlantic City. Some dumpy hotel." He waved his hand dismissively. "But the location is prime. I'm sure I can pick it up for a song."

"How can you be so sure? Atlantic City properties are not cheap."

"This one is. Besides, the owner has no idea I'm interested. If he did, the price would skyrocket."

Nonchalantly she asked. "How much do you think you can pick it up for?"

Alex laughed. "Two mil. But with what I plan to do with it, it's worth five times that amount."

Brigitte folded her linen napkin. "What's the name of that hotel?" she asked casually.

* * * * *

Chapter 20

Anne Turner sat at the coffee-stained marble table, a smoldering cigarette hanging from the corner of her pink mouth. She sighed and flipped impatiently through the thick pile of legal papers under the watchful eyes of her son. She paused and read one page slowly. Finally she looked up. "Are you sure this can work?"

He smiled confidently. "Absolutely."

She pulled the cigarette from her mouth and tapped it on the edge of the overflowing ashtray. "Even if it does work, it would take years. I don't understand why you don't want to confront him. You really don't need to go through all of this complicated legal stuff, you know. He owes us."

The young man hesitated. "Believe me. I know what I'm doing. When I'm through with Alex Ivanov, I won't be walking away with a measly couple of million dollars." He leaned back in the chair and folded his arms across his chest. "It won't happen overnight, but when I'm finished, I'll control Power Properties."

Anne Turner's pink lips broke into a smile. "I like the sound of that," she said and her blue eyes twinkled, allowing a brief glimpse of her former beauty. "I really like the sound of that."

* * * * *

Chapter 21

It had been one and a half years since David's death; six months since Brigitte's release from the clinic. During that time Alex had managed to stay a short step or two ahead of financial disaster. There had been no spectacular new success for Power Properties, no grandiose restorations, no major deals, only a few overpriced purchases of land and hotels and the constant and ongoing struggle to keep the creditors at bay.

The board of directors was gathered around the long mahogany conference table. The mood was palpably dark.

"Our best chance," was saying Gerald Masson, "is to go public. That's the only hope we have of raising the kind of money we need."

"We've already looked into that," replied Alex, morosely. "Besides, Power Properties has always been a privately owned company, and I'd like to keep it that way. But even if we wanted to, the process of taking a company public would take anywhere from a year to—" He shook his head, dismissing the idea. "—God knows when. We don't have that much time. The banks are breathing down our necks as it is."

From across the table, Natalia listened avidly, the heavily made-up eyes in the round face darting from Alex to Gerald. She leaned forward eagerly after Alex had spoken, and tapped the thick report resting on the table before her. "It's not too late. According to this report, the public has no idea of the problems we're having. Our reputation is solid. If we don't go public we can still try to find some investors. We all know how much the press loves us. All we need is a flurry of new publicity, some articles about the casinos or Power Properties Tower, and people will jump at the chance to invest.

Andrew, silent until then, broke into the discussion. "No way! Forget investors. The amount we need is too high. We'd only end up losing control of the company." He shook his head. "We're barely holding on as it is. Besides, even if we managed to get private investors on a debt rather than on an equity basis, it would only mean higher payments. We can't afford the payments we have as it is." He glared at Alex and continued coldly. "Why you had to buy those properties in Atlantic City, I really don't know. You paid top dollar for every one of them."

Alex interrupted. "I must admit it was uncanny how the owners held on until we offered the maximum I was willing to pay. It was almost as though they knew what we had agreed our top price would be."

Andrew continued. "I'm fed up with doing everything your way. Look at the mess you've put the company in."

Before anybody could respond to Andrew's statement, there was a knock at the door and a moment later Leonora Hart, Alex's private secretary rushed in.

"What is it Leonora?" asked Alex, irritated at the intrusion. When the board of directors was in a meeting, nobody was allowed to disturb them.

"Sorry to intrude," said Leonora, composed as always. Only the slightest tremor in her voice suggested her true state of mind. "We have a small problem at the front desk. That lawyer is out there again. He refuses to leave."

"What, again!" exclaimed Alex, impatiently.

"How many times has the guy been here? Doesn't he know by now that I don't want to see him?"

"He insists on having an appointment with you, sir. He says he has something personal to discuss with you."

"Oh for Chrissake. I don't have time for this."

"Sir, he's been here every day for the last three weeks. I don't know what to do with him anymore."

"Call security," said Alex. "Have him thrown out again, and this time warn him that if he ever sets foot in this building again, we'll have him slapped with a restraining order."

Leonora nodded, relieved. "Thank you sir. I didn't want to make that decision without your approval." She left as quickly as she had come in.

"Where were we?" asked Alex, as soon as the door had closed behind her.

"In deep shit Alex," replied Andrew. "In real deep financial shit."

* * * * *

In his mahogany-paneled office, Alex looked

out the window. From his vantage point high above Manhattan he could see clear across the city, all the way beyond the river to Brooklyn. *I'm on top of the world. That's a long way from the 'end of the world'*, he thought, remembering how he used to call Brooklyn as a child. *Now if I can just hold on long enough to get back on solid ground.*

For the nearly twenty-five years that Alex had worked and built his company into one of the most impressive real estate holdings in the world, it had often seemed as though he was only playing at a giant game of Monopoly; one at which he always won. But even more than the endless hours of hard work he had put into Power Properties, there had been one other factor he could not deny. Luck! *Like Natalia used to say, I have a horseshoe up my ass.* And indeed, for a long time, it had seemed that no matter what he did, Alex Ivanov could do never go wrong. Now, his luck had finally run out. During the last few years, every property he had purchased had been bought for top dollar. *How the hell did they always know exactly how high I was willing to go.*

Suddenly, the telephone rang, interrupting Alex's dark thoughts. He picked up the receiver and answered harshly. "What is it, Leonora?"

At the other end, Alex's secretary sounded

apologetic. "Sorry Mr. Ivanov, Sidney Elmsby of the First Country bank is on line four."

Alex took a deep breath and picked up line four. "Sidney," he exclaimed, carefully hiding his nervousness with an easy manner. "I haven't spoken to you in a long time. How are you?"

The president's voice came back dryly. "I'm fine Alex. The question really, is how are you? I'm told you've fallen behind in your payments again. I don't think I need to tell you how unhappy that makes me. I'm afraid I have to ask you to come and see me at your earliest convenience."

Alex felt his stomach tighten. "Sure Sidney. Let me take a look at my calendar and I'll give you a shout back."

There was a moment of silence at the other end of the line. Then Sidney Elmsby's voice came back, more insistently. "I'm afraid that's not good enough Alex. Unless we meet before your next payment is due, in two weeks, the First Country bank will have no choice but to start proceedings to seize Power Properties' assets."

"Sidney, you have nothing to worry about," Alex said reassuringly. "Let me take a look at my calendar and I'll get back to you." After Alex had put down the receiver, the telephone rang again immediately. He picked it up angrily and almost shouted. "What is it now Leonora?"

"He's here again, the lawyer." There was a tremor to her voice.

"For Chrissake, Leonora. How many times do I have to tell you? Why are you bothering me with this? Call security. Have him thrown out."

"Sir, I would," she answered, in a gruff whisper. "But he's handcuffed himself to me."

"What!" For a second, Alex had a vision of Leonora Hart, the indomitable secretary of steel, in a situation over which she had no control. The thought was ludicrous, and for a moment Alex almost forgot about his problems. He chuckled.

Leonora continued with barely controlled irritation. "With all due respect, this is not funny, sir. He says he won't unlock them unless you agree to grant him a five minute interview."

"I'm coming right over," Alex answered, suppressing his amusement. The sight of Leonora Hart handcuffed, was one he did not want to miss. He slammed down the receiver and strode purposefully down the long carpeted hall to the reception area.

Behind the elegant reception desk, Leonora sat stiffly in her fashionable black Chanel suit, an expression of fury on her impeccably made-up face. She was flanked on her right, by a handsome and well-dressed young man. Except for the anger on the secretary's face, one would never have guessed that anything was amiss. "What the hell is going on here?" asked Alex, his anger resurfacing at the sight of the young man who had been hounding him for weeks.

"Sir," came the young lawyer's nervous reply. "I'm sorry that I've had to resort to such lengths to get your attention, but I had no other choice. I tried everything else I could think of."

"You know I could have you arrested for this?"

The young man continued earnestly. "I-I know sir, but if you'll only give me five minutes. After that, if you still wish to have me arrested, go ahead. Five minutes, that's all, and I'll never bother you again."

Alex paused for a moment and looked at him. He was hardly more than a boy. There was nothing sinister about him. If anything, he seemed to be a pleasant, well mannered type. Alex's eyes quickly swept over him and took in the well-tailored clothes, the conservatively-styled black hair over the strongly chiseled features and the bright, intelligent clear blue eyes. For some reason, there was something hauntingly familiar about the young man.

"What's your name?" asked Alex, wondering briefly whom he reminded him of.

"Richard Conrad, sir," the young man answered nervously.

Next to him, Leonora was fuming. "Sir, can you please make him release me?"

Alex ignored his secretary's outburst and addressed himself to her captor. "You have a lot of nerve, Richard Conrad," he said. "Five minutes. That's all."

Those were the words Richard Conrad had waited to hear. He beamed as he pulled out a key from his pocket and quickly unlocked the handcuffs.

As they came off her wrist, Leonora pulled away abruptly and picked up the telephone. "I'll have security here in two seconds sir," she said as she began to dial.

Alex put up a restraining hand. "Hold on Leonora. I promised the man five minutes, and he'll get them." Without another word, he strode back to his office. Richard Conrad hesitated for a moment, and then hurried after him.

As soon as the door had closed behind them, Alex spoke quietly but fiercely. "I have no idea what you think you were doing out there, but let me tell you this. As far as I'm concerned, you have been harassing my staff for months, and now this. Are you aware, Mr. Conrad that handcuffing yourself to Mrs. Hart is tantamount to hostage-holding? That is a criminal action and you—if you really are a lawyer—should know damn well better than to do something as stupid as that."

Richard Conrad blanched. "I-I understand what you're saying, sir and yes, I am a lawyer. I graduated from Harvard two years ago and passed my board exams. I worked hard for my certification and, believe me I would not have acted as I did if I could have thought of any other way to get your attention." He struggled for words again and continued. "Your secretary was never in any danger from me. I am not a violent man. I apologize if I frightened her."

Alex sat behind his desk and nodded toward the chair across from his. "Have a seat. Your five minutes started," he glanced at his watch, "two minutes ago."

Richard Conrad pulled himself a chair and set his briefcase on the smooth surface of the desk. "Sir," he said. "Let me start by saying that for the past few years, I have taken an interest in Power Properties and I have studied this company thoroughly. I have read every article, every financial report. I have followed its progress and made my own analysis of your situation." He paused for a moment, looked Alex straight in the eye and continued. "I am fully aware of all your financial problems, sir."

Alex forced himself to remain calm. *If this is some extortion attempt...*

"And I have, what I believe sir, to be a solution to your problems."

Alex chuckled. "Not that I'm admitting to any problems, but do you really expect me to believe that some hot-shot snivel-nosed lawyer can come up with a solution that our board of directors, with their years of combined experience, could not?"

"Let me explain." The young man opened his briefcase and pulled out a thin folder. He leaned forward eagerly in his seat, no longer a nervous young man, but a calm and confident lawyer. "According to my analysis, the company is dangerously overextended. Every single property you have has been overvalued by as much as fifty percent and is mortgaged by as much as seventy percent. Technically speaking, sir, you are bankrupt." He let his words sink in before continuing. "It is only a question of time before the banks catch on and start their actions against you. Oddly enough, your greatest advantage is the fact that your debts are so enormous that, rather that seize and find themselves with no other choice than to write off your loans, the banks will be willing to do just about anything to give you a chance to pay them back."

Alex sat back in his chair and folded his arms across his chest. To his surprise, this kid was right on every detail of his assessment. *How the hell did he get his information?* He wondered.

"And what exactly is the solution you propose?" he asked quietly.

"Take Power Properties public," Richard answered with a triumphant smile.

There was a moment of tense silence before Alex began to laugh. "That is your solution? I'm afraid it is not very original, and certainly not plausible. Even supposing you were right about our financial problems, do you have any idea how long and how complicated it is to take a company public? If Power Properties really was in trouble, we would need a fast solution, not one that would take years before it brought about any results."

Richard Conrad's smile did not waver. "Sir, have you ever heard of a reverse takeover? For the next few minutes, he quickly outlined his plan.

* * * * *

As soon as Richard Conrad left, Alex called Natalia into his office. Natalia arrived, huffing and puffing. Alex swiftly closed the door behind her. He waited until she eased her weight into the cushions of the long leather couch and began. "I want you to look into something for me, and I don't want anybody else to know about this." For the next fifteen minutes he gave her all of the information he had.

At the end of his briefing, Natalia shook her head in wonder. "I don't understand. This Richard Conrad must have spent years working on this. He couldn't possibly have learned the specific details about Power Properties without having access to privileged information. Who the hell is he? And what does he really want from you?"

"That, my dear," replied Alex. "Is what I'd like you to find out for me. You still have more connections than anyone I know."

Natalia smiled and fluttered her false eyelashes at the compliment. "Except for you," she said. "But I suppose you don't want your name mixed up in this. Am I right?"

Alex nodded. "Oh. And by the way, would you look up some company by the name of Better Tools and Dies, while you're at it?"

"What the hell does it have to do with Richard Conrad?"

"Again, that's what I'd like to find out. Also, I know this is a long shot, but find out if there is any relation between Richard Conrad and Andrew."

Natalia was stunned. "Our Andrew?"

Alex looked uncomfortable for a moment. "Andrew and I seem to be having problems lately."

"Still, Alex! You can't possibly imagine..."

"One thing I've learned my dear. Never imagine anyone to be above greed and malice. Human nature is a bitch."

Natalia was silent. "I feel sorry for you, Alex." She struggled to heft herself out of her seat. At the door she turned around. "I'll get the information for you by Friday."

* * * * *

Four blocks away, Richard Conrad walked into the coffee shop of the San Moritz Hotel and looked around for a moment. Across the room, he spotted the familiar head of blond hair and hurried over.

The woman waited until he gave her the perfunctory kiss on the cheek. "So how did it go?" she asked, as soon as he was seated.

Richard kept his face impassive. "Where's the menu? I'm starving."

"How can you think of food at a time like this? Tell me how it went," she ordered, almost shrieking.

Richard leaned back in his seat, pulled a Camel from his mother's package on the table in front of him, lit it, and took a long drag. "I got his attention."

Anne Turner hesitated for a moment, not daring to believe it could have been so easy, and then she laughed.

Richard exhaled slowly. "From here on, it's a walk in the park."

• • • • •

Chapter 22

The report Natalia compiled was impressive. She gave Alex a quick overview a few days later in his office. "Richard Conrad graduated summa cum laude, the youngest in the history of Harvard's faculty of law. He passed his board exams the following year while working as an assistant to the D.A. in New York. In his two years as a prosecuting attorney, he won six of his seven cases. His hobbies are tennis and women. He is quite a playboy and his name has been linked to..."

Alex interrupted sharply. "I'm not interested in his sex life. What I want to know is who is he? Where does he come from? What is his financial situation? His family might be connected. Who are they and who do they know?"

"I was coming to all of that," replied Natalia, and she continued her briefing. "And by the way, I found no link whatsoever between him and Andrew." Alex had the grace to look embarrassed. Natalia continued. "His father was Harold Conrad. Conrad made his money in the clothing business and retired very comfortably after marrying Richard's mother. He passed away, broke, a few years ago. His widow had to sell the house, her car and all of her jewelry to send Richard to Harvard." Natalia closed the file and shrugged. "From what I could gather, Richard's mother led somewhat of a wild life until she met her husband. It seems she had a number of wealthy lovers, but nobody I could identify. As for Richard, he is reputed to be a bright, determined and ambitious lawyer." Natalia stopped and waited for Alex to comment.

Alex drummed his fingers on the leather pad of his desk. "He sounds almost too good to be true, doesn't he?" he asked. "What about Better Tools and Dies?"

"From what I could gather, the company is legitimate and Richard Conrad is not associated with it in any way. It was founded thirty-three years ago by Melville Hammer, and he took it public ten years later. For a long time it did very well, but lately the stock has fallen to a fraction of what it used to be worth. It seems that Melville

Hammer tried to regain control of the company and bought back most of the stock. Unfortunately, he nearly ruined himself in the attempt. He has no more capital to invest in his tool production and the company is tottering on the edge of bankruptcy." She paused for a moment, waiting for Alex to react. "What are you going to do?" she asked.

Alex hesitated, and then shrugged. "I've looked into Conrad's idea, and it seems that it could work. Maybe, just maybe, Richard Conrad is a blessing in disguise. I don't see how I have any choice but to go with his plan and hope to hell we pull it off."

* * * * *

"So?" said Richard Conrad a few hours later in Alex's office. "Have you thought of my proposal?"

Alex leaned forward and opened the folder on his desk. "I have taken the liberty of preparing a contract for you. If you want to take a look at it..." He handed the papers over to Richard. "I think you'll find it very generous."

Richard read through the typewritten sheets quickly. Then, his expression inscrutable, he put them back on the desk. "I'm sorry," he said. "But I can't accept this."

"What?" Alex was aghast. "That is more than I've ever offered anyone to come and work for me. What exactly do you want?"

"I want a vice-presidency," replied Richard calmly. "And you can't afford not to give it to me."

Alex looked across his desk, quietly assessing the young man. In his experience, he had never come across such brash confidence before. *That's who he reminds me of,* he thought with a shock, and smiled. *He reminds me of myself when I was his age.* "You have a lot of nerve, Richard Conrad," he said. "A hell of a lot of nerve. I like that."

"Thank you sir," replied Richard Conrad. "I got that from my old man."

• • • • •

A few days later, as the board of directors filed into the conference room, Gerald and Andrew stared with curiosity at the handsome young man sitting next to Alex. As soon as everyone was seated, Alex began the meeting. "I would like all of you to welcome Richard Conrad into our company. Richard is joining Power Properties as the newest member of this board. As of today, Richard is our vice-president in charge of legal affairs."

There were gasps from Andrew and Gerald. For a moment they looked at Richard with suspicion.

Alex continued. "Richard Conrad is a lawyer, graduated summa cum laude from Harvard. I have personally made a few inquiries about him and even though his reputation is solid and his references impressive, those are not the reasons I have decided to hire his services. Richard seems to have come up with a solution to our problems." Alex paused for a moment and turned to the young man. "Richard, why don't you explain?"

Richard cleared his throat and began. He talked about his long interest in Power Properties and his analysis of the company's financial situation. He briefly outlined the different ways the company might have chosen to find new capital and the numerous reasons why those traditional methods would not have worked.

From across the table, Andrew McGregor was growing impatient with Richard's speech. "We already know about our financial problems," he said. "And we also know what we can't do, but we still haven't heard anything that explains why Alex unilaterally decided to give you a vice presidency."

Richard Conrad continued without a pause. "The solution is to go public, but not in the traditional way. What I propose is a reverse takeover." Richard hazarded a glance across the room and was met with more suspicious looks. He continued. "A reverse takeover is when a small company buys out a large company, rather than the other way around. And if that small company also happens to be public, the big company automatically becomes public also." As he spoke, he could see the skepticism in everyone's eyes gradually change to curiosity. "I have located a small tool and die company that has been registered on the New York stock exchange for a number of years, and because it has been showing steady losses for the past five years, trading has all but stopped and the stock has become relatively worthless. Worthless, that is, to anyone but us," he added with a smile.

Alex took over the rest of the explanation. "I have also taken the liberty of buying, in all of our personal names, the corporate shell of Better Tools and Dies. I have received permission from the bank to allow Power Properties to sell all of its assets to this public company for one dollar. The bank will of course, still hold the loans and mortgages on all of the properties, even though they will be under the new corporate shell."

Gerald looked stunned. "How in Heavens did you manage to get the bank to agree to that?" he asked.

"As Richard very astutely pointed out to them," explained Alex. "Now that the price of real estate has plummeted, we owe them more money than our properties are worth. They can't afford to see us go bankrupt. By allowing us to go public, they are only protecting their own interests."

"Are you saying that from now on we'll have to go under the name of Better Tools and Dies?" asked Andrew.

"The name Power Properties now belongs to the new corporation. It was just a matter of a few maneuvers for Better Tools and Dies to legally adopt the name of Power Properties."

There was another long silence in the room. Natalia was the first to speak. "That," she said, "is brilliant."

Suddenly everyone was speaking at once. "What about the existing shares of Better Tools and Dies?" asked Gerald.

"There are probably thousands of people sitting on them all over the country. How can we expect to keep control of the company if we don't know where all of those shares are?" continued Andrew.

"Can you imagine the flurry of activity on the stock exchange when this goes public?"

"We have to make sure word of this doesn't get out. Everyone will be snapping up shares before we're ready."

Alex held up his hands and everyone quieted down. "The beauty of this is that the shares of Better Tools and Dies were almost exclusively held by the owner of the company, and he has agreed to sell them to us along with the corporate shell. Granted, there are a few loose shares floating around, but the total doesn't amount to more than thirty per cent."

"How much did all of this cost us?" asked Gerald.

Alex smiled with satisfaction. "Five hundred thousand dollars."

Andrew let out a low whistle. "How did you manage that?" he asked.

"Richard handled the negotiations," replied Alex.

"And I was acting for an anonymous firm," continued Richard with a bright smile. "The owner of Better Tools and Dies has no clue who I was negotiating for. If they'd had any idea we were behind this, they would have held out for millions."

Andrew chuckled. "I would love to be there when he finds out Richard was acting for us. Sounds like Richard has been taking private bluffing lessons from you, Alex."

Alex smiled benignly. "I hate to admit it, but I think I might learn a thing or two from Richard. He concocted the whole plan himself."

With a little help from my mother, thought Richard Conrad. *With a little help from Anne Turner.*

* * * * *

Chapter 23

Brigitte had never felt so happy and so frustrated all at the same time. She watched Gerald sitting across from her on the back patio of his home. She loved him just as much as he loved her. Of that she was sure. When they were together, they could barely keep their hands off each other, and for the first time in over twenty years, she felt wanted.

They had just spent a leisurely afternoon making love and she was still glowing in its aftermath. *Gerald is everything I've ever dreamed of in a man. He must leave Power Properties*, she thought. That fact had become a sore point between the two of them.

Alex was in no position to buy Gerald out and

she could not leave her husband as long as they were working together. But there was one other reason Gerald had to leave Power Properties, a reason she could not share with anyone.

She pushed back her cup of coffee. "Alex told me that he's taking the company public," she said casually. "I think that if you want to leave, now would be the perfect time. Alex will have the liquidity to buy you out. Or, you can simply sell all of your shares. So far we've managed to keep our relationship a secret, but God only knows how long we can keep up this charade. "

Gerald groaned. "You've got everything figured out, haven't you?"

"Well of course, I think..."

"And I wanted to surprise you with the news myself." He laughed. "Drink your champagne. It'll lose its bubbles."

She took a sip of her coffee and looked at him suspiciously. "You wanted to surprise me?"

He smiled. "Drink your champagne."

Brigitte frowned. "Gerald! Don't play games with me. Tell me."

He shook his head. "I'll tell you just as soon as you finish your drink."

She smiled. "You're teasing me." She picked up her glass, drained it in one long gulp, and almost choked. "There was something in my glass," she said and pulled it out of her mouth. "Wh-what!" For a moment she did not know what to think. She was staring at a beautiful emerald-cut diamond ring. "Gerald..."

Gerald watched the stunned expression on her face and laughed. "I know you won't be able to wear it openly until everything is settled, but what do you say? Will you marry me?"

* * * * *

Anne Turner strolled leisurely through Saks' fur department, brushing her hand sensuously along the pelts of the hanging coats. A saleswoman in a tight skirt and an equally tight smile hurried over. "Can I help you?" she asked in a dripping voice.

Anne pulled herself tall and flicked her mane of blond hair with a lazy hand. "I'm just looking, thank you."

The pleasant look on the sales-woman's face immediately morphed into one of condescending superiority. "There are no sales in this department. If you're looking for bargains, I suggest you try another department."

Be nice to me, bitch! Anne wanted to shout. *Or you just might lose out on some heavy commissions. I may not be spending any money today, but I will be soon.*

Her pleasure spoiled, Anne Turner turned away and hurried out of the department. Why Richard would not allow her even the smallest shopping spree, she could not understand. The money was as good as theirs already. "Fool!" she told herself sharply, and two women standing by the elevator turned to stare at her. She ignored them and took the stairs. *Why do I wait for him to tell me what to do?* His plan was brilliant. She did not understand all of the details, but the bottom line was that they would soon be very rich. The thought thrilled her and she laughed with merriment, her voice echoing through the stairwell.

As she walked out of Saks, she was happily dreaming up dozens of ways of spending all that money.

* * * * *

When the news of the reverse takeover became public one month later, the reaction was exactly as Richard Conrad had predicted. The stock opened at two dollars a share in the morning. At closing it had already quadrupled. Within the week, it had jumped to twelve. One month later, it was trading at twenty-eight and was still climbing.

Alex made the announcement to his board of directors two months later. "I think we should look into Atlantic Airways. I hear they're having some financial difficulties. How does Power Air Lines sound?" he asked.

Across the table, Andrew's face turned a deep shade of crimson. "Alex, for Chrissake, we just pulled ourselves out of financial trouble by the skin of our teeth. You overpaid for every one of the properties you've bought lately. We won't show a profit on those until five or six years from now. We need to strengthen our financial position. Now is not the time."

Natalia raised a painted eyebrow. "Andrew," she said. "Haven't you learned by now? Save your breath. When Alex sets his mind to something, he doesn't let go. He'll find a way."

Richard looked worriedly at Alex. "Sir, with all due respect, I think Andrew is right. I don't think we can afford to buy an airline right now. We're only starting to recover from our difficulties."

Alex nodded. "Maybe so, but let's not throw this idea out until we've looked at every angle. What do you say, Gerald?"

Gerald had been sitting quietly until then. He looked up. "I don't think my opinion is needed here." For two months now, he had been waiting for the moment. This was it. He gathered his courage and continued. "I'm leaving Power Properties."

"You're what!" Alex was stunned.

Now that he had said it, Gerald felt relieved. "I want to retire. I've worked hard for many years and now I want to be able to relax and enjoy my life. This is something I've been thinking about for a long time, but until now I didn't see how you could possibly buy me out."

Alex was speechless. He knew, just as everyone else in the room, that Gerald had made up his mind. "I—I don't know what to say."

Gerald shrugged. "Don't say anything. Just buy me out."

Alex thought quickly. "Under one condition; wait until the deal with the airline is done. Just a couple of months, that's all. Otherwise Power Properties loses what could be the opportunity of the century."

"Gerald, Power Properties just won't be the same without you," said Natalia, tears glistening behind her false eyelashes. "Don't leave."

Alex saw his hesitation, and pushed again, gently. "Just two months Gerald. Two months, that's all I'm asking."

Gerald struggled with himself. He had already waited for so long, two months was not much longer. He wondered briefly if Brigitte would understand and felt a pang of guilt. "Two months," he said finally. "Two months. Not one day more."

• • • • •

Anne Turner held the silk dress tenderly in front of her and threw an admiring glance at her reflection in the bedroom mirror. *Yes, this dress will definitely do.* She hung it in the closet and returned to her purchases, strewn across the bed. She carefully unwrapped each one; shoes by Charles Jourdan, scarf by Hermes and earrings from Tiffany's. She had even bought herself some First perfume along with the body lotion, the soap and bath oil. *So what if I bought myself a few things? Soon I'll be filthy rich*, she told herself, thus dismissing any guilt she might have been feeling. *Richard might have his own plans for Power Properties, but I have plans of my own; plans my son knows nothing about.*

She gently folded the Hermes scarf, walked across the room to her dressing table and carefully placed it in the top drawer, right next to the small pearl-handle revolver her husband had bought her years ago. She picked it up and caressed the smooth handle. There was a time when she had considered using the gun. The image of Alex Ivanov lying in a pool of his own blood had given her immeasurable pleasure. *That would have been too easy*, she thought bitterly as she placed the revolver back into the drawer. *This plan is much better.*

* * * * *

CHAPTER 24

William Brandon was sitting at his mahogany desk, smoking his eternal cigar, when the call came in. "William Brandon," he answered gruffly. The voice at the other end of the line was unfamiliar. "Who is this?" he asked and nearly dropped his cigar when the answer came. "What?" Memories flashed through his mind as he listened.

Over the last twenty-five years, William Brandon & Company had undergone considerable change, as had its owner. As his multi-million dollar company dwindled, William Brandon watched his girth expand and his hair disappear. He had become an old and bitter man.

A few months after his affair with Ann Turner

had ended so many years ago, his wife, suddenly and without explanation, asked for a divorce. Bill was stunned. "Why?" he wanted to know. He had left his mistress. Wasn't that what his wife had wanted?

It was only minutes before their case was scheduled to be heard that the real reason became clear. From across the crowded courtroom hallway, Cornelia strolled over and leisurely dropped a brown manila envelope in her husband's lap. With trepidation, Bill tore it open. Inside were dozens of pictures of him and Anne Turner in little more than their birthday suits, and engaged in activities that could be best described as clearly unprofessional. "Where did you get these?" he asked as sweat broke out on his forehead.

"Does that really matter?" his wife asked back. Then she smiled a tight, vicious, little smile. "May I suggest you agree to the settlement my lawyers are asking for, or I will make sure these pictures have as wide a circulation as the *New York Times*."

"But why? I don't understand."

"Why?" she repeated. "Darling, these pictures are worth a fortune, and frankly, I wouldn't mind a fortune of my own right now. I spent a quarter century being your wife and raising our children, and look at what that got me. You were willing to drop me in a second for a blonde hussy half my age." She smiled bitterly. "I'm only looking out for myself. Finally."

The divorce was granted that same day and it cost William Brandon nearly half of all he owned. His wife's lawyers had left the courtroom with barely-disguised self satisfaction. No small wonder, they had earned twenty percent of five million dollars in less than four hours.

Bill had driven back to the Plaza damning the day he ever laid eyes on Ann Turner. This was all her fault. Hers and Alex Ivanov's.

Over the years, Bill Brandon had almost forgotten about Anne Turner and Alex Ivanov. Then one day, he picked up his usual copy of *TIME* magazine and there was Ivanov, smack on the cover. The press had trumpeted about his success with his Power Hotel and Casino.

The voice on the telephone continued with icy calmness "What I am offering is the opportunity to crush Alex Ivanov and Power Properties in one easy shot. You are interested, aren't you?"

The question was nearly rhetorical, of course. "Yes, I'm interested."

The voice at the other end of the line chuckled. "Of course you are, so this is the plan..."

William Brandon listened with avid curiosity.

* * * * *

The woman walked into "Yellow Fingers," the inexpensive lunch place near Bloomingdale's. She looked across the busy restaurant, recognized the head of sparse hair and briskly walked over. "Sorry I'm late. I hope you didn't think I stood you up."

William Brandon laughed and his belly rolled. "I knew you'd show up," he said as he pulled the envelope from his pocket. He handed the check over to the woman and she glanced at the figure with appreciation.

"Nice," she said, and slipped the six-figure check into her Hermes purse. She handed him the brown manila envelope. "How do I know you will follow all of my directions?"

"How do I know you aren't selling me a lot of hot air?"

She hesitated, her hand still on the envelope. "I guess we'll just have to trust each other."

Bill Brandon nodded. "I guess so." He felt her let go of the envelope and he grabbed it. "All I can say is that your demands are very reasonable. Nobody will know about this. As far as the other request, I have no problem with keeping the same board of directors. All except Alex!"

"All except Alex," she repeated and smiled.

The man took a sip of his Bloody Mary and another puff of his cigar. "But there is one thing," he said. "I know this is none of my business, but why are you doing this?"

The woman smiled as she clicked her purse shut. "You're right! It is none of your business." She turned and walked away.

• • • • •

Gerald had asked Brigitte to meet him for lunch at one of their favorite restaurants. They sat in a quiet booth in the back of the restaurant and ordered veal piccata and white wine. Brigitte glowed with anticipation. "So how did Alex react when you told him?" she asked eagerly.

Gerald sighed. He had dreaded telling her, but now he had no choice. "I've agreed to stay another two months," he admitted.

"What!" Brigitte was stunned. She pushed her

plate away and tears welled in her eyes. "I don't believe this. Two months, that's crazy." She was so upset, she was trembling. "I thought we had agreed that you were leaving Power Properties immediately. Gerald, I don't want to wait anymore. This is enough. Tomorrow you can go back and tell them you've changed your mind."

"Sweetheart, calm down. It's just another few months. We've already waited this long. What difference can eight weeks make?"

"It can make all the difference in the world. Gerald, promise me. Tomorrow you'll go back and tell them no."

Gerald was stunned at the vehemence of her reaction. "I can't do that," he said. "I gave them my word. If it was only Alex it might be a different story, but I have to think of Natalia and Andrew too. I don't want to let them down." He looked at Brigitte, puzzled. "What are you afraid of? Do you think I'm trying to back out of my promise to you?"

Brigitte bit her lip. "No, of course not it's just that..."

"Just what?"

Brigitte was struggling to control herself, trying to find the words. *How can I tell him that this will ruin everything? How can I tell him that his whole future depends on him leaving now?* "I-I guess it will be all right," she said.

* * * * *

Alex listened to the ringing at the other end of the telephone. "Ivanov residence, good afternoon," Réjeanne's familiar voice answered.

"Réjeanne, can I speak to Brigitte?"

"Oh, I'm sorry, Alex. She's not here. She went out after lunch and I haven't seen her since."

Alex sighed. For weeks now, he had been calling daily to check in on his wife, and every day Brigitte was out. In the back of his mind, a thought occurred to him. *Could she be involved with someone?* And just as fast, he dismissed it. *No, not Brigitte. She's probably just out shopping again.* "Thanks, Réjeanne. I'll see her when I get home." He put down the receiver and wearily rubbed his hand over his face. At that moment Andrew popped his head in the door.

For once his attitude was not hostile. "Alex, don't let me disturb you. Do you have any idea where Gerald might be?"

Alex looked up. "Isn't he in his office?"

Andrew shrugged. "No, I haven't seen him all afternoon. Yesterday was the same thing."

"He has been a bit scarce around here lately. If I see him, I'll tell him you're looking for him." He waited for Andrew to leave, and then he picked up the telephone again. "Leonora, tell me something. Is it my imagination or has Gerald been spending less time around the office lately?"

Leonora's voice came back, thoughtful. "He has been leaving earlier than usual lately."

"Any idea what he's been up to?"

At the other end of the line, Leonora chuckled. "I have the feeling he's seeing someone. Haven't you noticed how he's been walking around smiling? I think the man's in love."

Alex put down the receiver. For a moment he was too surprised to think. Gerald was seeing someone? Gerald was in love? Alex grinned. *Well the old son of a gun!* It was about time.

* * * * *

Later that evening, when Brigitte came home,

Alex was in bed reading the latest stock report. "You're home late tonight. Tired?" he asked as he put the report on the night table.

"Exhausted. I had meetings all day for the epilepsy foundation," she said as she crawled into bed. Over the past few months, she had invented half a dozen activities that needed her time. She leaned over and gave her husband a quick kiss on the cheek. "How is Power Properties doing?"

"Very well. The stock is up to thirty-three dollars a share. We're going ahead with the airline deal."

"That's wonderful," she said unconcerned as she turned away. "Good night." A moment later, she was asleep.

Alex listened to the sound of her breathing for a few minutes. He considered trying to make love to her. It had been so long since the last time. He tried to remember when, and what it had been like, but he couldn't recall. Memories of random mistresses through the years wandered through his mind. He fell asleep before retrieving the memory he sought.

. . . . .

Andrew McGregor barged into Alex's office unannounced. Alex looked up, surprised. "You look like hell. What's wrong?" he asked, noticing the expression of doom on Andrew's face.

Andrew threw the stock report on his desk. "Take a look at that."

Alex read the paper and blanched. He looked up. "What do you think that means?" he asked, already guessing the answer. His stomach was in a knot.

"It can only mean one thing. Somebody is trying to sandbag us."

"Who?"

"I have no idea," replied Andrew.

For a moment both men were silent. "Call a board meeting immediately," ordered Alex. "We'd better look into this right now."

Fifteen minutes later, the board of directors was assembled in the conference room. Alex spoke with icy calm. "I think we might be in for a rough ride. Somebody has been buying up large chunks of Power Properties stock. It looks like the first step toward a hostile takeover bid."

"Who do you think it could be?" asked Gerald.

"It could be anyone. There's no way of knowing until we complete the research."

"If they are serious, I wouldn't be surprised if they did much of the buying in the name of dummy corporations. I doubt the research will tell us anything," continued Gerald Masson calmly. "I only wish we hadn't stretched ourselves so thin with the purchase of Atlantic Airlines. Now we don't have the available cash to start buying more shares ourselves."

Alex felt his stomach tighten up again. "What we have to do is make sure that all our investors hold on to their stock. Meanwhile..."

"Alex," Gerald insisted. "We don't have the capital to buy back any large blocks of our stock, if that's what you're thinking. Don't forget, we all had to dilute our shares considerably when we went public."

"I know you were planning to leave in a few weeks, but whatever you do, don't dump your stock now, Gerald. That would kill us."

"How much stock does the bastard already have?" asked Natalia from across the table.

Andrew waited for Alex to answer. When he didn't, Andrew spoke for him. "We estimate that he holds approximately twenty per cent of the stock. And that is a conservative estimate. He could have been buying under a few other company names."

"Oh my God, what are we going to do?" asked Natalia.

Alex thought for a moment. Then he spoke. "Whoever this is, he hasn't made himself known yet, and the legal minimum for the offering period is twenty business days. That means that even if he made his offer tomorrow, we have three weeks to prepare. Meanwhile, I suggest we go on the biggest publicity blitz we've ever had. We are Power Properties," he said. "Not only the single most prestigious company in the country, but also the fastest-growing." He paused and thought quickly. "Natalia, I want you to update the list of shareholders. I think we should have a special evening for them, remind them of everything we have accomplished and give them a glimpse of what we're planning for the future. With any luck, we'll be able to prevent them from selling out. As far as I know, twenty per cent of a company is not enough for a takeover. We and our stockholders will still hold eighty." It was an inspirational speech, but four pairs of eyes stared back at him unconvinced. It was a known fact that the odds of preventing a well-planned and well-financed hostile takeover were only one in five.

"We'll have to move fast," said Natalia, breaking the silence. She was already heaving herself out of her chair. "I'll book the ballroom of The Pierre for the first available date."

"I'll help you get the updated version of the shareholder lists," said Andrew as he rose from his chair.

"Richard, I want you to look into preparing our strategy. We have a maze of anti-takeover defenses woven into Power Properties Holding's bylaws."

"I'll pull our corporate charter," said Richard as he hurried out.

Gerald Masson sat quietly. This whole takeover business was ruining his plans. Now he had no choice but to sit tight for another few months. "Isn't it interesting," he said as soon as he and Alex were alone. "How the timing of this takeover was so well planned."

Alex stopped and looked at Gerald piercingly. "Do you really think the timing was planned?"

"Do you really think it was a fluke?" replied Gerald. "Now, of all times—when I'm scheduled to leave the company, and when we've just made the single largest purchase in the history of the company. Power Properties has never been so cash poor."

"Only the board of directors had access to that information," said Alex softly.

Gerald cocked his finger at Alex. "Bingo! You just read my mind," he said.

* * * * *

CHAPTER 25

The weeks flew by in a flurry of preparations and strategy meetings and suddenly it was the day of the shareholder gala. Now that there was no more time, no more plans to put into effect, Alex felt overwhelmed with fatigue. He and his board of directors had worked harder than ever, reassuring stockholders, squelching rumors everywhere and during all that time trying to find out who was behind the takeover bid. Alex glanced at his watch. *Four o'clock.* It was time to go home and get ready.

Just as he was leaving, Natalia barged in. "What is it, Natalia?" he asked wearily.

Natalia crossed the room without a word and dropped into the chair across from his desk. "The switchboard just lit up like the fourth of July. He's just made his bid."

Alex sat back down. "Who is it?" he asked, dreading the answer.

Natalia shook her mass of blond hair. "I don't get it. I've never heard of the man. It's someone by the name of William Brandon. Have you ever heard of him?"

Alex's eyebrows shot up. "William Brandon!"

"He's offering forty-two dollars per share."

Alex leaned back in his chair and closed his eyes. "William Brandon. He must be a hundred years old by now. What the hell does he want with me?"

"This William Brandon, is he someone you stepped on?"

For a moment his chest felt unbearably tight. Then, just as suddenly as it had come, the pain passed. "Stepped on?" he said.

"Alex, you've built yourself a fortune, an empire. You stepped on a lot of toes and made a lot of enemies along the way. This is personal, isn't it?"

"How much time have we got before we need to show up at The Pierre?" asked Alex, disregarding Natalia's question.

"Five, maybe six hours." Still Natalia waited for a moment. Then she sighed and struggled out of her chair. "I guess we'd better get to work. If a dozen share holders got the offer, you can be sure they all did."

Natalia noticed a look of pain pass on Alex's face. "Are you all right?"

"I'm fine—just an upset stomach. Is everybody still here?"

Natalia nodded.

"Call an emergency meeting," continued Alex. "We'd better take another look at our strategy for tonight."

· · · · ·

Anne Turner was suspicious. She was also extremely nervous. For nearly three weeks she had been leaving message after message for Richard and still he did not call back. *What is he up to? If he is trying to cut me out of this deal...* She slammed down the receiver one more time and stood there, tapping her long red fingernails on the table. *Damn him*, she muttered to the mirror in the front hall as she grabbed her purse and stormed out.

She taxied over to his apartment in a huff and banged on his door. "There you are," she screeched when he finally opened the door. She was about to launch into a litany of abusive language when she realized that Richard was wearing his tuxedo. "Where, the hell, are you going, all dressed up like a penguin?"

"Nice to see you too, Mother," replied Richard as he walked back into his apartment, leaving the door open. Anne strode in behind him.

"What the hell is going on? And don't bother telling me that I'm imagining things. For weeks now, I've known that something has been going on at Power Properties, but you won't tell me anything about it. And don't imagine that you're leaving here until you do."

"In that case, make yourself at home. You might be here for a while."

Anne followed Richard to the bedroom as he knotted his bow tie. "Listen here you dumb jerk. I'm your mother. Don't start acting up with me."

Richard spun around and glared at her. "The only reason I haven't kept you up on what's been happening is that it is very important that everything remain confidential right now. The success of everything I've worked for depends on it."

Anne's eyebrows shot up. "So something *is* going on. What is it?" She waited expectantly. "Hey, I'm in this too you know. I've been very patient, letting everything go your way."

Richard finished knotting his tie and for the first time he noticed the expensive new clothes his mother was wearing. "I see you've been shopping. Where did you get the money?"

Anne looked guilty for a moment. "I got myself a few credit cards." She shrugged. "Don't try to change the subject. What's going on?"

Richard turned away. "We have a problem. This afternoon Alex found out that somebody by the name of William Brandon is trying to take over Power Properties. Tonight Alex is going to give a speech to all of the shareholders in the hope of keeping their vote."

Anne felt the blood drain from her face. "I think you'd better tell me all about it."

When Richard finished telling her the story, Anne was stunned.

"Mom, are you all right?" Anne's calm was almost eerie.

"Yeah! Sure! Don't worry about me," answered Anne, shrugging. She got up from the couch and picked up her designer handbag. "I think I'll go home now."

"You do that," replied Richard, as he escorted her to the door. "I'll let you know what happens as soon as I find out myself."

Half an hour later, Anne let herself into her apartment, headed straight for the liquor cabinet and poured herself a double Scotch. *I can't let William Brandon ruin everything*, she mumbled to herself. *I've waited too long for this and I refuse to let anyone stand in my way.* She nursed her drink for a while as her mind spun furiously.

* * * * *

That evening when Alex walked into the ballroom of The Pierre Hotel, resplendent in his tuxedo, he appeared radiant with unabashed confidence. He had chewed on half a dozen Rolaids and felt slightly better. He plastered a confident smile on his face and walked through the tables with Brigitte on his arm. The crowd of shareholders was already pleasantly mellowed by endless glasses of champagne, and the noise was that of a successful party in full swing. Music played softly in the background while waiters rushed about.

Alex stopped for a moment and looked

around. "This is it, sweetheart," he said to Brigitte, and took her by the elbow as he escorted her to the head table. *Tonight*, he thought, as he helped his wife into her chair and looked around at his vice-presidents, *I am giving the best performance of my life*. The performance had nothing to do with the speech he was about to give. *One of you has been leaking information to my enemy.*

"Are you ready for your speech, Alex?" asked Richard as he leaned over.

"Ready as I'll ever be." Alex took a deep breath and turned toward the dais. "Richard, do me a favor. Get me a Scotch. I have a feeling I'll need it when I come back."

Alex finished his speech and the applause came thunderously. He stood on the podium while the familiar velvety voice of Frank Sinatra's New York, New York filled the room. On the screen behind him, flashed publicity pictures of Power Properties real estate projects. He looked into the room and recognized some of the faces. There was Andrew, standing near the front talking to the mayor. Behind him was Brigitte chatting with a woman he thought he recognized. A moment later he spotted Richard and Natalia in a lively discussion with the host of a television morning show.

A feeling of dizziness swept over him. He grabbed the edge of the lectern to steady himself. The anxiety came rushing back and with it, the same tight sensation in his chest that he had felt earlier. Shit, the handful of Rolaids he'd taken earlier should have done the job. He stepped off and shouldered his way through the glittering crowd. "Great speech Alex," someone shouted in his ear and clapped him on the back. He smiled and nodded, grateful that nobody could guess how awful he felt. Under his tuxedo jacket, his shirt was soaked. He restrained the almost overwhelming urge to loosen his bow tie and kept his confident smile plastered on. The comments he heard along the way to his table were positive. "He's made the company what it is, why would I...?" someone said close by. "Whoever that Brandon guy is, he..." The rest of the sentence disappeared in the noise.

He returned to the head table where Richard congratulated him. "Great speech Alex." He handed him a glass. "Here, I got you that scotch you asked for." He watched as Alex downed the drink in one quick shot.

"Good stuff." Alex said, setting the glass down. "At the price the Pierre is charging me for for this ballroom, I guess the least I can expect is a good glass of Scotch." He looked around, and some of his nervousness dissipated.

The room looked stunning. Three large crystal chandeliers hung from the ceiling, their Austrian crystal lit like millions of candles. Fresh flower arrangements decorated the center of each table and everywhere, white-gloved waiters rushed about pouring endless glasses of champagne. Even the Plaza's ballroom, with the millions Trump had pumped into the place, could not rival the Pierre's.

"For a while there, I thought you'd forgotten what you wanted to say," said Richard.

"To tell you the truth, I don't know how the hell I pulled it off. I'm still not sure what I said up there," answered Alex, his smile still in place. He leaned over to Brigitte, and kissed her on the mouth.

"Congratulations Alex," she said. Alex, always the showman, pulled her up to her feet and into his arms for a passionate embrace. A few people from nearby tables cheered.

He released her just as Natalia joined them.

"Hey, Alex, you did a good job up there. I think it's in the can," she said, heaving her weight onto one of the fragile chairs. Luckily it held. Alex sat and leaned in close to her. The aging movie star was the only member of his board he trusted completely. She was, after all, the only one who had no reason to hate him.

"Who do you think is behind this," he asked.

Natalia returned his gaze with surprise. "I don't understand what you mean. We know who's behind this, Alex. It's William Brandon, who else?"

Alex shook his head, vehemently. "No. I've thought about it and there are just too many coincidences. The timing for one thing." He leaned in closer. "I think it's one of us."

Natalia scowled. "Don't be ridiculous."

Alex chose not to argue. He nodded instead.

"You're probably right." He could not afford to let his emotions show. *Whoever you are, you bastard, I'll find out and I'll make you pay.*

Alex turned back to Brigitte. She had been his wife for over a quarter of a century, almost half his life. Without her unwavering love and devotion during all those years he would never have had the energy to build Power Properties. She looked up at him, and he suddenly realized how beautiful she still was. *A beautiful stranger.* Sadness swept over him. *What is wrong with me?* he wondered, unused to feeling emotional. He tried to push away the thought that nagged in the back of his mind. *Maybe losing Power would not be such a bad thing. I could spend some time with Brigitte. Get to know her again. Would she even want to?*

He tried to remember the last time they had made love, but couldn't. It had been way too long. *I'm like king Midas*, he thought, remembering Brigitte's words from long ago. I built a fortune, but lost all the people I loved most.

He felt old and tired. He had alienated too many people during his life, some of them people he truly cared for. Now Brandon was trying to steal Power from him. *It's too late. I will never be able to recapture what was.* Brigitte smiled at him and he saw only indifference in her eyes. His heart lurched.

A wave of exhaustion hit him and suddenly he wanted to be anywhere but there.

"Let's get out of here," he yelled to Brigitte above the racket. She nodded and Richard Conrad jumped up to follow them. Alex said a quick goodbye to the others and opened the way to the entrance of the ballroom. He went down the curving stairs of the rotunda with Brigitte, followed closely by Richard.

Alex put his arm around her and hurried her on. "Why are we leaving so soon?" asked Brigitte, nervously "I would have thought you'd want to stay and speak with a few of the shareholders."

"I have a better idea" replied Alex.

"There's a lot riding on this, Alex. I don't know if it's such a good idea to leave now. We could lose a fortune," said Richard.

"Nobody knows that better than I do, Richard. You don't have to tell me how to run my business," Alex shot back gruffly. "I built this company. Nobody wants to keep it more than I do."

From above, the last words of Sinatra's' song carried out to them—something about making a brand new life.

They entered the lobby. A doorman noticed them and rushed over. "Can I get your car Mister Ivanov?" he asked. Alex handed him the parking stub. The man turned and rushed out.

Brigitte turned to Richard, and said, "Can we give you a lift?"

"No thanks. My apartment is just a couple of blocks away. I can use the fresh air," he answered.

Alex started saying something and stopped, a strange expression on his face.

"Are you alright, Alex?" asked Richard.

"Just some indigestion," he replied as his face began to redden and beads of perspiration rolled down the sides of his face. "Brigitte do you have a handkerchief or something?"

She opened her bag and handed him a Kleenex. "Are you all right? You don't look well."

"I'm fine, just fine. Probably something I ate." He wiped himself with the tissue and shoved it in his pocket. "Just a bit of upset stomach."

At that moment a black Mercedes pulled up, and the doorman hopped out. Alex held the door open for Brigitte, then went around and climbed behind the wheel. A minute later the car roared off.

• • • • •

Richard watched the taillights until they disappeared into the night. Why Alex sometimes insisted on driving his own car, he would never understand. With the amount of money that man had, he could afford a whole fleet of cars and drivers. One thing was sure, given half the fortune the old man had, he would have his own limo and never drive himself again.

He glanced at his watch. After the events of the Evening, he felt wide awake, full of energy. If everything went according to plan and they squashed the takeover attempt, he would soon be a very rich man. What an exciting thought. It filled him with feelings of exuberance, greed and lust, all jumbled together, sending a surge of adrenaline through his veins. It would be impossible to sleep tonight.

A woman, that's what he needed. He wondered briefly if he might be able to entice one over to his place. At this time of night, it would not be easy. Not too many women would go for the idea of a tumble in bed without the required wining and dining. For some unfathomable reason, some females seemed immune to his dark, movie-star looks. This normally presented Richard with what he enjoyed most, a challenge. But tonight he was not in the mood for a challenge. He wanted a hot and easy girl, not some tight-assed broad who would need hours of seducing before she came across. Then he remembered Sylvia. Hot and easy Sylvia. Whistling happily, he turned toward Fifth Avenue and walked home.

* * * * *

The traffic was light and the roads were smooth. The speedometer registered a steady eighty miles per hour.

Brigitte watched her husband with curiosity. "Now, can you tell me why we're going home so early?"

"No reason. I just needed to get out of there." He sounded irritated. As though reading her mind, he softened his tone and continued. "How is it going sweetheart?" In the dark he could just make out her profile, and the rich red of her hair looked almost black. The sequins on her dress sparkled every few seconds from the reflection of the city lights. He guessed, more than saw, the smile she gave him. He reached over and affectionately covered her hand with his.

"I'm fine," she replied. There was no warmth in her voice.

"God it's hot in here. Mind if I turn on the air conditioner?" He fiddled with the control on the panel and settled back with a sigh of satisfaction as the cold air began to blow. "Do you still love me?" he asked, and Brigitte looked at him in surprise.

"What a strange question," she replied uneasily and laughed. "Are you feeling all right?" She stopped and looked at him as he suddenly began breathing heavily. "Alex, what's wrong?" She unclasped her seat belt and tried to grab the steering wheel as the car swerved dangerously close to the median.

"My heart," he replied, gasping. Then, as she watched helplessly, he let go of the wheel and clutched at his chest. Frantic, Brigitte tried to loosen his collar while keeping one hand on the wheel.

She never saw the car as it came directly at them.

* * * * *

Chapter 26

The telephone rang insistently. Richard Conrad opened one bleary eye and noticed the blond hair spilling over the pillow next to his. *Sylvia*, he remembered and immediately regretted having called her. Now he would have to make small talk all through breakfast, and she would probably want to set another date before leaving his apartment. *Aw, hell! All I wanted was a quick tumble in bed, not a relationship.* The phone rang again interrupting his thoughts.

"Christ it's the middle of the night," he said under his breath.

"What time is it?" asked Sylvia sleepily as she reached a lazy hand over to caress his back.

"Four thirty in the morning," he said and picked up the phone. "Yes," he answered. "Yes, this is Richard Conrad." There was a long pause then suddenly he pushed away the bed covers and sat upright. "Where? How did it happen? Yes, yes, no problem. I'll be right there." He slammed down the receiver, jumped out of bed and quickly pulled on a pair of pants.

"Where are you going?" asked Sylvia as she watched him from the bed.

"To the hospital," he replied abruptly.

"Why? What happened?"

"None of your business," he answered, deliberately cold. "And by the way," he added as he finished buttoning his shirt "I don't want you here when I get back."

The pillow landed on the door just as he closed it behind him.

* * * * *

The hospital felt deserted so early in the morning. Richard hurried along the hall, his shoes squeaking on the green linoleum. He stopped at the information desk.

"I'm here about the Ivanovs."

The receptionist nodded and picked up the intercom. "Doctor Thomas to the front desk please. Doctor Thomas." The message echoed through the hospital on the intercom system.

"Can't you give me any information about their condition?"

"I'm sorry, I'm not allowed to give out any information. Here's the doctor now." She smiled apologetically and turned her back discreetly as the doctor approached. On the counter next to her was a small portable radio. She busied herself with the dial.

"Mister Conrad?" He extended his hand. "I'm doctor Thompson. I was the attending physician when the Ivanovs were brought into emergency."

"Yes, yes. How are they?"

The doctor hesitated for a moment and looked uncomfortable. He cleared his throat. "I'm afraid it isn't good…"

* * * * *

William Brandon, stark naked except for the

towel he wore draped around his neck, looked out of the window of his suite at the Plaza. Since his divorce, he had never bothered getting another house and moving out. After all, he no longer had a wife to care for his needs and the Plaza offered just as good a service as any woman could. He was the longest-paying customer in the history of the hotel and he felt proud, somehow, of that fact. It gave him an odd sense of belonging.

He leaned forward, squinting his puffy eyes. From his angle, he could clearly see the entrance of The Pierre Hotel, a stone's throw away. A moment earlier, he had watched with avid curiosity as a shiny black Mercedes had pulled up and an elegant couple stepped out. Although from his distance he could not tell who they were, he was convinced it was Alex and his wife. Now he took another drag from his cigar and smiled. *You just try and get out of this one*, he thought with smug satisfaction. At that moment, there was a knock at the door. "Just a moment," he called out and pulled the towel from his neck and wrapped it around his waist. "Who is it?"

"Room service."

"I didn't order room service," he muttered to himself as he opened the door.

One single shot rang out, pushing him with such force that he stumbled backward a few steps before he even realized he was hit. "Wh-what?"

The intruder watched calmly as he stumbled to his knees, and then to the expensive Oriental rug as blood spurted out of the small wound in his chest.

"Didn't anyone ever tell you not to open the door to strangers?" The intruder stepped forward quickly, placed the gun to Brandon's temple, pulled the trigger again, then stepped back, closed the door and hurried down the hall to the bank of elevators.

* * * * *

Chapter 27

Gerald arrived at the hospital, looking harried and disheveled. "How is she?" he asked, frantic. "I heard on the news. I came as fast as I could," he explained as the others stared at him.

Réjeanne, Richard, Natalia and Andrew sat in the private waiting room the hospital had made available for them. They all wore the same look of shock and disbelief.

For the third time since the Ivanovs had been brought in, Doctor Thompson patiently explained. "Mr. Ivanov had a minor heart attack. Luckily, he was brought to the hospital very fast and once we were sure he suffered no injuries from the crash, we gave him an injection of rTPA to dissolve the blood clot and help decrease the damage to the heart muscle."

Gerald nodded. "What about Brigitte?"

The doctor hesitated. "Unfortunately," he said. "Mrs. Ivanov has not been as lucky. The air bag was only on the driver's side of the car, and it seems she was not wearing her seat belt. When she was brought in, Mrs. Ivanov showed signs of massive internal bleeding. We operated and removed her spleen to stop the bleeding."

"So she'll be fine," he said, wanting very badly to believe it.

Doctor Thompson shook his head. "While we were inside, we found a tumor on one of her ovaries. The tumor was large, and when we removed it, we were unable to keep it intact. The ovarian capsule burst. If it was malignant, there may have been some seeding of the cancer cells inside the peritoneal cavity. Because of the bleeding in the area, we were unable to suction abdominal fluids for analysis."

Gerald, who had been standing until then, collapsed on the sofa. "Cancer! How can that be? She was perfectly healthy."

Doctor Thompson continued. "Any talk about cancer is still premature at this time. We won't know whether the tumor was malignant until we get the results from the lab." The doctor paused for a moment, and when the others did not ask questions, apologized and began to turn away. "I'm sorry but I have to get back to my other patients. As soon as I get the report from the lab, I'll let you know."

"Can I see her?" asked Gerald.

The doctor shook his head. "She's still in recovery and won't be able to see anyone for a few hours."

"This couldn't have happened at a worse time," said Andrew. "I wonder what this is going to do to the stockholders."

Gerald exploded. "Who cares about the fucking stockholders!"

Natalia, ignoring Gerald's outburst, answered. "We don't have to worry about the stockholders anymore."

"What are you talking about? With Alex in the hospital, they are sure to vote Brandon in," retorted Andrew glumly.

Natalia shook her head. "William Brandon is dead. He was murdered last night. I heard it on the radio on my way here."

Gerald's face blanked in shock as his thoughts left Brigitte momentarily. "Do they know who did it?"

"No. They mentioned something about unknown intruders."

Andrew groaned. "Who wants to bet that we will all be suspects?"

"The single most important thing we can do right now," said Natalia, "is make a show of strength and unity. We must put out a statement immediately. We can't afford a panic. Make sure to stress that Alex suffered only a mild heart attack and is expected to recover fully. Don't mention anything about Brigitte, except to say that she suffered some internal injuries and had to undergo some surgery. I don't want the word cancer to be so much as breathed to anyone. Do you understand? Make sure the hospital knows exactly what they can say. In the meantime, business goes on as usual."

After all of the others had left, Gerald Masson stood by the window and looked at the grey skies. This was like a bad dream. One he had already lived many years before. He remembered his wife and her long slow death after months of painful battle against ovarian cancer. Brigitte was the only other woman he had ever loved, and now she might suffer from the same affliction. *Dear Lord*, he prayed silently. *Don't take her away from me too. Not now. Not when we were so close to being together.*

* * * * *

When it came back from the lab, Doctor Thompson read the report quickly. He picked up the telephone and called Gerald Masson at Power Properties. "I have good news," he explained. "The tumor was benign."

Gerald felt dizzy with relief and for a moment he couldn't speak. "H-how is she?" he stammered.

"She's out of the anesthesia. You can go and see her now."

"And how is Alex?" he added as an afterthought.

"He's resting at the moment, but we've scheduled him for a series of electrocardiograms and angiograms over the next few days. He'll be in between procedures."

Forty minutes later Gerald walked into Brigitte's private room, carrying three dozen red roses. For a moment he stood in the doorway looking at her. She looked so vulnerable in her sleep, pale and motionless. There were tubes coming out of her everywhere. "Brigitte," he whispered as he came closer. "Darling, it's me."

Brigitte stirred and opened her eyes.

"I brought you some flowers."

She smiled. "I was just dreaming about you."

"Pleasant dreams I hope."

She nodded. "The doctor said we had an accident. I don't remember…"

"Shh. The important thing is that you'll be fine." He caressed her face with one free hand. "I also have good news for us. The takeover bid is over. William Brandon was murdered last night. That means I'll be free to leave Power Properties just as soon as Alex comes back."

William Brandon, dead. The words echoed in Brigitte's mind. She shook her head weakly, fighting the remnants of the anesthesia. *The takeover bid is over. Oh my God!* "Gerald, I want to tell you something…"

"Shh." Gerald put the flowers on the bedside table and leaned over. "I love you," he whispered.

Panicked, Brigitte struggled to keep her eyes open. "Th-there's something I have to t-tell..." But before she could finish, she was asleep again.

Later, when Gerald returned to the office, he was greeted by a panic-stricken Leonora. "All hell has just broken loose. The switchboard hasn't stopped for one minute. The stockholders are going crazy about Brandon and the takeover and about Alex being in the hospital. Reporters are calling every second, and to make matters worse, now there's someone from the police here. He wants to question everyone about William Brandon's murder."

"Tell the reporters we are preparing a press conference and that we will notify them of the time and place. In the meantime, you can reassure the stockholders that Alex is expected to make a full recovery and that business is going on as usual." He sighed. "I'll handle the cop. Where is he?"

"In the conference room."

Gerald strode down the hall. In the room, Natalia, Andrew, Richard and the inspector were gathered around the table. The inspector was a big man and dwarfed everyone except Natalia. He studied Gerald through annoyed eyes as he walked in.

Natalia spoke first. "Gerald, this is Inspector Lawson. He wants to know..."

Inspector Lawson interrupted. "William Brandon was murdered last night. He was shot sometime between seven and ten P.M. in his suite at the Plaza. I understand that he was making a run for Power Properties."

Natalia shook her head vehemently and her chins wobbled. "Yes, but we only found out it was him yesterday afternoon. And last night, we were all at the stockholder's gala between seven and ten."

"If you don't mind ma'am, I would like to ask the questions." Lawson pulled out a grimy pad and a pencil. "William Brandon was found by one of the hotel maids late last night. He was shot with a 22 caliber, one bullet in the liver from a few feet away and one in the head at close range."

"That sounds like a professional killing, doesn't it?" asked Natalia, eagerly.

Lawson looked up at her. "Not when the gun is a small caliber." He paused. "Brandon was making a run for this company and in my books, that's a motive for murder."

The partners looked at each other. Their silence acknowledged there was no arguing with Lawson on that one.

After the meeting, Lawson returned to the precinct. His partner hurried over before he had a chance to slump his weary bones down in the equally tired-looking chair behind his desk. Larry Miles was in his early thirties and looked like he should be playing quarterback for the Notre Dames. "So, how did the meeting with the big shots go?"

Lawson, disregarding the creaking of his old chair, leaned way back. He took a deep breath and exhaled noisily. "I don't know. I spoke to them together, and then questioned each one individually. Natalia Berenson, you remember her? The old movie star? She was a mess of nerves, but I have a feeling that's just her personality. On the other hand, Gerald Masson, he's got something he's hiding. Andrew McGregor hates Alex Ivanov. He feels that Ivanov has been stretching the company finances too thin. He might have wanted to murder Ivanov but why Brandon? And the young one, Richard Conrad..."

Miles interrupted. "Are you talking about the same Richard Conrad, who used to be with the DA's office?"

"The one and the same. He looked like he was going to be sick the entire time I questioned him." He sighed and put his feet on the desk, causing another series of ominous sounding creaks. "I think we should look into all of them, but concentrate on Masson and Conrad."

His partner smiled brightly. "Conrad, well I'll be. I wondered what happened to him. He used to think he was such a hot shot." He pulled out a plastic bag from behind his back. "Maybe we shouldn't disregard the movie star yet. Take a look at this." In the transparent bag was a gun. A small, 22 caliber, very dainty and feminine revolver.

Lawson whistled. "Where did you get that?"

"In the dumpster behind the hotel kitchen. I'm going to the lab to have it checked out right now."

When they came, an hour later, the results were definite. "I have good news and bad news," said Miles as he put down the receiver. "The good news is that the ballistics checks out. The bullets that killed Brandon came from this gun. The bad news is that the gun was not registered."

"Why did I know you were going to say that?" asked Lawson.

• • • • •

Chapter 28

Richard walked into his apartment and headed straight for the bar. He poured himself a double Scotch and swallowed it in one shot.

"You look like you have a problem," a voice said from behind.

Richard spun around, his heart already hammering in his chest. "Mother! What the hell are you doing here?" he asked angrily.

Anne Turner laughed. "What kind of a welcome is that?"

Richard slammed his glass on the bar. "How did you get in?"

"Now, now, don't get excited. I told the

superintendent that I am your mother and he very nicely let me in. I've been waiting for hours. Where've you been? "She walked over to the bar and using her son's glass, poured herself a drink."Hmm, good stuff," she said and turned back to face him. "I just heard the good news."

"What good news is that?"

"Oh Richard, sometimes I wonder about you." She smiled brightly, exposing two perfect rows of teeth. "The news about Brandon, of course. We don't have to worry about the takeover anymore, do we?"

Richard nodded wearily. "That's right. The takeover bid is dead, as dead as Brandon."

Anne laughed and swallowed another gulp of her drink. "Too bad Alex and his wife didn't die in the car crash at the same time, isn't it?" She walked across to the leather sofa and sat, draping her arms along the back. "Then," she continued thoughtfully. "You could have broken any will Alex might have, proven your birthright and inherited everything.

"There's no point in theorizing, Mother. Alex is still alive."

Anne leaned forward as the thought came to her. "You know, that is not a bad idea. You are, after all, vice-president in charge of legal affairs. I think you should suggest to Alex that he draw up a new will. Then, when it's ready for signing, all you have to do is make sure that he reads the original copy and have him sign a few—let's say—slightly improved copies, and destroy the one original." She threw up her arms in a victory sign. "Don't you think that's brilliant?"

"Don't you think someone might wonder why the lawyer who wrote the will got everything?"

Anne stuck out her lower lip in a childish pout and thought quickly. "I've got it." she exclaimed. "You could always argue that Alex knew all along that you were his son, that this was a secret between the two of you. The fact that he took you into the company would add weight to your claim. Nobody could argue differently."

"This is a stupid conversation. Alex is alive and will stay alive for a long time to come."

"Who knows? Accidents do happen. And don't forget, the man is over fifty, works like a dog and has a heart condition. I think you should take this idea very seriously." Anne smiled sweetly. "Very, very seriously."

• • • • •

Five days after the accident, the doctor removed Brigitte's catheter and gave her a brief examination. "I think you can go home in another few days," he said and scribbled on her chart. "You are one very lucky lady," he said as he left the room. "By the way, there's an inspector waiting to see you outside. I'll tell him that you can see him now."

Lucky, thought Brigitte. *What luck?* For months, she had carried out what she thought was the perfect plan. *Oh Gerald, if only you had sold your shares when you were supposed to.* Since the news of Brandon's murder, the stock had fallen by eighteen per cent, and now the police were here. *How could everything go so wrong?*

There was a knock at the door and a moment later it opened. "Brigitte Ivanov?"

Brigitte looked at the beefy looking man and her heart sank. "Yes?"

He walked over to her bed and pulled out a pile of cancelled checks from his briefcase. "I'm inspector Lawson and I'm looking into William Brandon's murder. Could you tell me why, in the last two months of his life, the victim wrote you checks for a total amount of nearly two million dollars?"

After he had left, Brigitte was exhausted.

There's no use pretending anymore. I'd better call a lawyer.

* * * * *

After his interview with Brigitte Ivanov, Lawson hurried over to the hospital coffee shop to meet with Larry Miles. Larry was already seated and was devouring a jelly doughnut. "Hey, you won't believe what I just found out," he exclaimed with his mouth still full. "Listen to this! Richard Conrad is Alex Ivanov's son."

Lawson looked at the document Miles handed him proudly. It was a birth certificate for Richard Ivanov.

"He was born out of wedlock to one Anne Turner, and was later adopted by her husband, one Harry Conrad. That is why his name is now Conrad." He leaned over and crossed his arms on the table. "Nobody at Power Properties mentioned any of this, did they?"

Lawson shook his head. "Nope."

"Wanna bet even Ivanov isn't aware of it?"

After Miles had left, Lawson realized he had

been so excited with his partner's news, he had forgotten to tell him about his interview with Brigitte Ivanov. *Damn! I can't believe I forgot to tell him this one.*

* * * * *

Alex was sitting up in his hospital bed, his face rigid with anger as he barked his orders to the doctor. "Don't tell me to relax. I am furious and I have every right to be. I'm fine and I want to be released now. I have a business to run and unless you do as I tell you, I will sue you and the hospital for any losses my company suffers while you are holding me here against my will. Do I make myself clear?"

Doctor Applebaum, a short thin man with a round balding head, nodded. "Perfectly clear, Mr. Ivanov. Now if you will just calm yourself, I'll get your release forms ready immediately." He turned and walked out. Before the door could close completely, it swung open again and a delivery man walked in.

"And who the hell are you?" shouted Alex.

"Are you Alex Ivanov?" he asked unnecessarily. Alex's face was almost as well known as the United States president.

"Yes."

"This is for you. Sign here." The young man handed him an envelope, and walked out.

Alex tore open the envelope and pulled out a sheaf of paper. For a moment he thought his eyes were wrong. This couldn't be. No, this had to be some kind of mistake. It was just not possible. *Brigitte is suing me for a divorce!*

He climbed out of bed and into his slippers and bathrobe. Seconds later, he was hurrying down the hall when Louise, his day nurse, stopped him. "Where do you think you're going like that?"

"I'm going to see my wife," he shot back.

She grabbed him by the arm and pulled him back toward his room. "Oh no, you're not. You can't walk out of this ward."

"I want to see my wife, and I want to see her now," he yelled.

"Fine, but you'll have to go by wheelchair," she answered.

"I'm not crippled, dammit! I can walk."

"I'm sure you can, but hospital rules." She hurried across the hall and reappeared moments later with the chair.

I'm not a fucking invalid, thought Alex. I'd rather die than be stuck in one of those, thought Alex morosely.

There was no arguing Louise when her mind was made up. She helped Alex into the chair and smiled. "Now, which floor is your wife on? I'll push."

Minutes later, Alex was wheeled into Brigitte's room. Brigitte closed the book she had been reading. "Hello Alex," she said calmly.

"I would like to speak to my wife privately," he said. The nurse left the room and closed the door discreetly behind her.

When they were alone, Brigitte spoke. "Did you get the papers?" For some reason, she was feeling none of the nervousness she had anticipated. Instead, she was calm and sure of herself.

Alex felt his breath suck out of him. *So it's true*. He tried to speak. "Why?" he asked hoarsely.

"How can you even ask?" The calm she had felt a moment ago was gone. Now she was angry. "After all the affairs you've had, you dare to ask me why?"

"But that was a long time ago..."

"How dare you lie to me? You've had so many affairs I don't think you can even remember them all. Did you really think I didn't know?" She laughed. "You gave them the same Fred pendant you gave me for our tenth wedding anniversary."

"B-but... I've changed. All of that is over. You must believe me. I haven't had an affair since..."

"Since David died!" Brigitte shouted, and suddenly she was calm again. "David, whom you forced to take swimming lessons, David, whom you killed, just as surely as you killed my career; just as surely as you killed any love I ever felt for you." She paused again, and took a deep breath. "Let it go, Alex. It's over. I am divorcing you."

Alex felt his chest tighten.

Before he could say anything, Brigitte continued. "Oh, and one more thing. I might as well tell you myself, before you hear it from the police..."

"Wh-what?"

"I was the accomplice working with William Brandon for the takeover. I remembered how you told me that he was in real estate development and how he hated you. I'm the one who thought up the takeover plan and I approached him. Every one of the properties you bought in Atlantic City, he bought before you and sold you at double, triple and quadruple the price he paid. My share was ten per cent and the satisfaction of screwing you, the same way you screwed with my heart." With that, she opened her book and began to read. "Goodbye Alex."

Alex struggled to speak, but his voice was gone. He tried to move but his body would not cooperate. The pain in his chest had radiated down his arm and through his back. "Arrrh..." he gurgled.

Brigitte looked up. "Oh my God!" She reached for the call button and began to push frantically.

• • • • •

Chapter 29

When Anne Turner heard the news, she became frantic. She tried desperately to reach Richard at Power Properties, but he had already left. *I just hope he was smart enough to take my advice.* She kept calling Richard's apartment all evening, until finally, around midnight, he answered.

"I just heard the news about Alex. Did you make out his new will like I told you?"

"Alex is still alive, mother."

"I know! I know! But did you make out his new will?"

Richard hesitated. Sometimes she drove him crazy. The last thing he wanted was to get into an argument with his mother. "Yes, yes I did."

He heard her sigh of relief. "Thank God for that. I wouldn't want Alex to die without his new will."

For a long time after, Richard lay in bed thinking. *Why do I have the feeling she expected him to die?*

· · · · ·

Alex's second heart attack was more severe than the first, and for a week he remained in intensive care, hooked up to a heart monitor. After his condition had stabilized, he underwent a double by-pass operation which, the doctors reassured him, would give him the heart of a twenty five year old.

· · · · ·

After the news that Alex would recover, Brigitte had been so overcome with relief that she could not stop crying. "You have nothing to feel guilty about," said Gerald once again. "It isn't as though you tried to kill him. You simply told him that you were leaving him. How were you supposed to know he would have a heart attack?"

Brigitte was sitting in her hospital bed, her face buried in her hands. "That's not all I told him," she said through her tears. "I told him that he killed David."

Gerald tried to put his arms around her but she pushed him away. "Sweetheart, I can't say that I blame you for that. I'm just surprised you never exploded before."

"There's something else. Something I haven't told you." Brigitte watched Gerald's face as she spoke. "I also told him that I was the one who gave Brandon all the information." Gerald looked at her in disbelief. "I was behind the takeover bid, Gerald. It was me."

• • • • •

Lawson walked into his office and tapped on the window to Miles' office next door. A moment later, Miles walked in carrying two Styrofoam cups of coffee. "So, what have you found out?"

Lawson was thoughtful for a moment while he tore the cover off his cup. "The only person who could have done it, is Conrad. It seems he left the gala with the Ivanovs at nine o'clock and according to the doorman, he refused a lift with them. He wanted to walk back to his apartment. It would have taken him no more than ten minutes to get to the Plaza and ride up the elevator, or walk up the stairs to Brandon's room."

"Do you think he really did it?"

Lawson shrugged. "We know that the movie queen, Masson and McGregor were at the party until after midnight. Alex and his wife were on their way home. There's nobody else, unless it was a professional hit." He shook his head. "And this was no professional hit. It has all the marks of an amateur." He paused again and took a sip of his coffee. "We could build a pretty good case on circumstantial evidence."

Miles nodded slowly. "There's only one problem. You remember him in court. He was one hell of lawyer. You can bet your ass that he'll build himself one hell of a defense and if all we have is circumstantial evidence, we won't stand a chance in hell of nailing the bastard."

* * * * *

The interrogation room was familiar to Richard. It was small, eight feet by ten, furnished with a long narrow table and a few chairs. He knew that the mirror on the wall was a one-way window and he wondered briefly if anyone was watching now.

He had watched countless suspects be interrogated in that very room during his years with the DA. Nevertheless, being on this side of the table was not nearly as pleasant. He wiped his moist palms on his trousers and willed his heart to calm. He'd be damned before he showed any concern. He forced himself to sit back and appear relaxed. "I could insist on my lawyer being here," he said with a smile that belied his tremulous position. "I don't have to answer any of your questions."

"We're aware of that," answered Miles. "But on the other hand, why would you need a lawyer? We're only trying to solve a case and we think you could help us."

Lawson pointed to the tape recorder. "You don't mind, do you?"

Richard shook his head.

Lawson waited until the tape was spinning. "Why didn't you ever tell Ivanov that you are his son?"

Richard felt his heart skip a beat. "No comment," he replied.

Lawson watched for a reaction. "You say you went straight home after you left the gala that evening. Is there any way you can prove that?"

"No comment," replied Richard again as his heart hammered in his chest. *If only Sylvia had arrived before midnight. She could have been my alibi.*

Miles pulled a small box from across the table and opened it. "Did you ever see this gun before?" he asked as he pulled it out.

For a moment Lawson thought he saw something in Conrad's eyes. What was it? Surprise? Fear?

"No comment," answered Richard once again.

• • • • •

Anne Turner was sitting at her makeup table, giving a last coat of polish to her nails, when the doorbell rang. "One moment," she called out as she walked to the door, blowing on her fingers. "Oh, it's you," she said.

Richard pushed her aside and strode in. "You killed him, didn't you?"

Anne tossed her hair with a shake of her head and looked at him innocently. "I don't know what you're talking about."

"Don't play games with me, Mother. You killed Brandon, didn't you? I was just questioned by the police and they showed me the murder weapon."

For a split second she looked frightened. Then just as quickly, she recovered. "What did you tell them?" she asked.

"Nothing yet, but let me tell you something. If I could figure it out, so can the police."

Anne remained impassive. "Well, then I suggest you be my alibi. Otherwise, I could claim that you were my accomplice."

"You bitch!"

Anne looked at her son in bewilderment and shook her head. "I really don't understand you at all. Brandon was going to ruin everything. I only did what I had to do to protect you. If Brandon had taken over Power Properties before Alex died, we would have lost everything."

Richard stared at his mother in horror as the realization hit him. "Jesus Christ! You're planning to kill Alex, aren't you?"

Anne laughed. "Sometimes you really are slow," she answered. "Did you think I would wait until that bastard died of natural causes?" She strolled to the sofa and patted the seat beside her. "I've got it all planned, and this is what we'll do."

* * * * *

Alex was lying in his hospital bed, watching the small television screen overhead when the nurse came in. "Good morning Mr. Ivanov."

He looked up in surprise. She was an attractive middle-aged woman with blond hair pulled back in a tight bun. "You're not my regular nurse," he said. "Where's Louise?"

"I'm taking over for Louise today. We switched schedules." She smiled. "It's time for your medication." She handed him the paper cup and Alex brought it quickly to his mouth. "And here is your water," she said sweetly as she handed him the glass.

Alex picked up the glass and drank it.

Suddenly, the door to the adjoining bathroom swung open and Miles rushed out. "You're under arrest," he shouted as he pointed his gun to Anne Turner.

Behind him Lawson hurried over to Alex. "Are you all right Mr. Ivanov?"

"Sure," replied Alex with a grin. He opened his palm, revealing the three capsules he had pretended to swallow.

• • • • •

Epilogue

Sometimes Alex wondered what would have happened if Richard had not gone to the police with his story. Would he have died that day? *No. I would have been suspicious*, he told himself. *Louise would have told me if she had changed schedules.* Luckily, that was something he would never know for sure. *I don't think I'll ever die*, he reassured himself again. After all, he had evaded death five times already. He's had two heart attacks, a car accident, a murder attempt, and now this.

"Would you like me to move your chair closer to the window Mr. Ivanov?" asked his manservant.

"No, I can see fine from here." Alex leaned back in his wheelchair and looked out the window.

Shortly after Anne Turner's arrest, Alex had suffered a third, massive heart attack. From now on, the doctors told him, he would no longer be ambulatory. Since then he had been bound to this damned chair.

It gave him some consolation to know that he had a son, and that this son had saved his life. *See? Not everybody hates me*, he thought. *Richard cares for me.* On the strength of Richard's testimony, Ann Turner had been convicted and sentenced to eight years in jail. *He testified against his own mother because he loves me.* But Richard had not come to visit in nearly a month. *He's busy running Power Properties. He doesn't have time.* But Power Properties headquarters were only a few floors below the penthouse in Power Tower, where Alex now lived.

Andrew and Natalia had not come to visit in a long time either. *Gerald I can understand. Since he married Brigitte, I couldn't really expect him to keep in contact.* Alex turned his head and looked at the painting on the wall. It was a stunning oil of an orchid, modern yet classic, bold yet peaceful. When he heard that Brigitte was painting again, he had sent Sam to the gallery to buy it for him. *I hope she's happy*, he thought, already knowing the answer. He had caught a glimpse of his ex-wife on a television interview just before her first showing, and she had seemed to glow. *She looks happier than I ever remember seeing her.*

"Sam," Alex called out. "I've changed my mind."

Sam came running. *And well he should, for the money I pay him.* "Move me closer to the window. A bit more to the left." *Ah, this is better.*

From his vantage point, he could see clear across the city, all the way to Brooklyn. *To the end of the world*, thought Alex, remembering how he used to call it when he was a kid. "I made it, didn't I Sam?" he asked.

"You sure did, Mr. A."

"Everything I touched turned to gold."

Sam nodded. "You're a regular King Midas, Mr. A."

Alex laughed. "You know, somebody told me that once…a long time ago. But all I am is a Scorpio, that's all. Did you know Scorpios are the most ambitious sign in the Zodiac, Sam?"

"I can't say that I knew that, Mr. A."

"But I was ambitious, wasn't I, Sam?"

"That's for damn sure, Mr. A. That's for damn sure. Why…with all your money, you must be the happiest man in the whole world, Mr. A."

The End

Made in the USA
Charleston, SC
20 October 2011